THREE THOUSAND DOLLARS

Stories by

DAVID LIPSKY

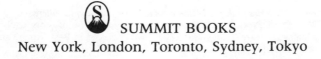 SUMMIT BOOKS
New York, London, Toronto, Sydney, Tokyo

Summit Books
Simon & Schuster Building
Rockefeller Center
1230 Avenue of the Americas
New York, New York   10020

SUMMIT BOOKS and colophon are trademarks
of Simon & Schuster Inc.

Designed by: H. L. Granger/Levavi & Levavi
Manufactured in the United States of America

1   3   5   7   9   10   8   6   4   2

Library of Congress Cataloging in Publication Data
Lipsky, David
Three thousand dollars : stories / David Lipsky.
p.   cm.
Contents: Three thousand dollars—Lights—"Shh"—Near
Edgartown—Relativity—Answers—Colonists—World of
airplanes—Garden—March 1, 1987—Springs, 1977.
I. Title.
PS3562.I627T47   1989
813'.54—dc20
89-11392
CIP
ISBN 0-671-67346-7

*Some of the stories in this collection have appeared, in slightly different form,
in* The New Yorker, Mississippi Review, *and* The Boston Globe
Magazine. *"Three Thousand Dollars" was included in* Best American
Stories 1986.

For my mother, and
for Lisa Ryan

CONTENTS

THREE THOUSAND DOLLARS   9

LIGHTS   29

"SHH"   41

NEAR EDGARTOWN   59

RELATIVITY   69

ANSWERS   121

COLONISTS   137

WORLD OF AIRPLANES   159

GARDEN   177

MARCH 1, 1987   189

SPRINGS, 1977   201

THREE THOUSAND
DOLLARS

MY MOTHER DOESN'T KNOW that I owe my father three thousand dollars. What happened was this: My father sent me three thousand dollars to pay my college tuition. That was the deal he and my mom had made. We'd apply for financial aid without him, to get a lower tuition, and then he'd send me a check, and then I'd put the check in my bank account and write one of my own checks out to the school. This made sense, not because my father is rich but because he makes a lot more money than my mother does—she's a teacher—and if we could get a better deal using her income instead of his, there was no reason not to. Only, when the money came, instead of giving it to the school, I spent it. I don't even know what I spent it on—books and things, movies. The school never called me in about it. They just kept sending these bills to my mother, saying we were delinquent in our payments. That's how my father found out. My mother kept sending him the bills, he kept looking on them for the money he'd sent me, and I kept telling him that the school's computer was making an error and that I'd drop by the office one day after class and clear it up.

So when I came home to New York for the summer my mother was frantic, because the school had called her and she couldn't understand how we could owe them so much money. I explained to her, somehow, that what we owed them was a *different* three thousand dollars—that during the winter the school had cut our financial aid in half. My mother called my father to ask him to send us the extra money, and he said that he wanted to talk to me.

I waited till the next day, so I could call him at his office. My stepmother's in finance, and she gets crazy whenever money comes up—her nightmare, I think, is of a river of money flowing from my father to me without veering through her—so I thought it would be better to talk to him when she wasn't around. My father has his own advertising agency now in California—Paul Weller Associates. I've seen him at his job when I've visited him out there, and he's pretty good. His company does all the ads for a big western supermarket chain, and mostly what he does is supervise on these huge sets while camera crews stand around filming fruit. It's a really big deal. The fruit has to look just right. My father stands there in a coat and tie, and he and a bunch of other guys keep bending over and making sure that the fruit is okay—shiny-looking. There are all these other people standing around with water vapor and gloss. One word from my father and a thousand spray cans go off.

When he gets on the phone, I am almost too nervous to talk to him, though his voice is slow and far off, surrounded by static. I ask him to please send more money. He says he won't. I ask why, and he says because it would be the wrong thing to do. He doesn't say anything for a moment, and then I tell him that I agree with him, that I think he is right not to send the money. He doesn't say anything to acknowledge this, and there is a long pause during which I feel the distance between us growing.

Just before he gets off the phone, he says, "What I'm

really curious about, Richard, is what your mother thinks of all this," and this wakes me up, because he doesn't seem to realize that I haven't told her yet. I was afraid to. Before I came home, I thought of about twenty different ways of telling her, but once she was right there in front of me it just seemed too unbearable. What I'm afraid of now is that my father will find this out, and then he will tell her himself. "I mean," he says, "if I were her, I probably couldn't bear having you in the house. What is she planning to do? Isn't the school calling you up? I can't imagine she has the money to pay them. Isn't she angry at you, Rich?"

I say, "She's pretty angry."

"I hope so," my father says. "I hope she's making you feel terrible. When I talked to her on the phone yesterday—and we only talked for a couple of seconds—she seemed mostly concerned with getting me to give you this money, but I hope that deep down she's really upset about this. Tell her it's no great tragedy if you don't go back to school in the fall. You can get a job in the city, and I'll be happy to pay your tuition again next year. I'm sorry, but it just doesn't feel right for me to keep supporting you while you keep acting the way you've been acting, which to me seems morally deficient."

My mother is tall, with light hair and gray, watery eyes. She is a jogger. She has been jogging for six years, and as she's gotten older her body has gotten younger-looking. Her face has gotten older, though. There are lines around her lips and in the corners of her eyes, as if she has taken one of those statues without arms or a head and put her own head on top of it. She teaches art at a grammar school a few blocks up from our house, and the walls of our apartment are covered with her drawings. That's the way she teaches. She stands over these kids, while she has them drawing a still life or a portrait or something, and if they're having trouble she sits down next to them to show them what to do, and usually she ends up liking her own work so much that she brings it home with her. We have all these candlesticks and clay flowerpots that she made during class. She used to teach in Greenwich, Connecticut, which is where we lived before she and my dad got divorced, which was right before I started high school. Every summer, she and a bunch of other teachers rent a house together in Wellfleet; she will be leaving New York to go up there in six days, so I only have to keep her from finding out until then.

When I get off the phone, she is in the living room reading the newspaper. She gives me a ready-for-the-worst look and asks, "What did he say?"

I explain to her that I will not be going back to college in September. Instead, I will be staying in the apartment and working until I have paid the school the rest of the money.

My mother gets angry. She stands up and folds the paper together and stuffs it into the trash. "Not in this apartment," she says.

"Why not?" I ask. "It's big enough."

"A boy your age should be in college. Your friends are in college. Your father went to college. I'd better call him back." She walks to the phone, which sits on the windowsill.

"Why?" I ask quickly. "He said he wasn't going to do it."

"Well, of course, that's what he'd say to you. He knows you're afraid of him." She sees I'm going to protest this. "Who could blame you? Who wouldn't be afraid of a man who won't even support his own son's education?"

"He said he doesn't have the money."

"And you believe him?" she asks. "With two Volvos and three bedrooms and cable TV? Let him sell one of his cars if he has to. Let him stop watching HBO. Where are his priorities?"

"I'm not his responsibility."

"Oh, no. You're just his son, that's all; I forgot. Why are you protecting him?"

I look up, and my mother's eyes widen a little—part of her question—and it feels as if she's seeing something in my face, so I realize I'd better get out of the room. "I'm not protecting him," I say. "It's just that you always want everything to be somebody's fault. It's the school's fault. It's nobody's fault. It's no great tragedy if I don't go back to school in the fall; you're the only person who thinks so. Why can't you just accept things, like everyone else?" I walk into my bedroom, shutting the door behind me. I lie on my bed and look up at the ceiling, where the summer bugs have already formed a sooty layer inside the bottom of my light fixture. My ears are hot.

Our apartment is small. There are only the two bedrooms, the living room, the bathroom, and the kitchen, and so if you want to be alone it's pretty impossible. My mother comes in after a few minutes. She has calmed down. She walks over to the air conditioner and turns it on, then waves her hand in front of the vents to make sure that cold air is coming out. I sit up and frown at her.

She sits down next to me and puts her arm around my shoulders. "I'm sorry you're so upset," she says. As she talks, she rubs the back of my neck. "But I just think that there are a lot of things we can do before you have to go out and look for a full-time job. There are relatives we can call. There are loans we can take out. There are a lot of avenues open to us."

"Okay, Mom."

"I know it must be pretty hard on you, having a father like

this." She gives me time to speak, then says, "I mean, a man who won't even pay for his son's school."

"It's not that," I say. "It's not even that I'm that upset. It's just that I don't want us to be beholden to him anymore. I don't even like him very much."

My mom laughs. "What's to like?" she says.

I laugh with her. "It's just that he's so creepy."

"You don't have to tell me. I was married to him."

"Why did you marry him?" I ask.

"He was different when I met him."

"How different could he be?"

My mother laughs, shaking her head. Her eyes blank a little, remembering. She was twenty when she met my father—a year older than I am now. I imagine her in a green flannel skirt and high blue knee socks. "I don't know," she says, looking past me. "Not very." We laugh together again. "I don't know. I wanted to get away from my parents, I guess."

"Who could blame you?" I say, but I can tell from a shift in her face that I have pushed too far. Her father died two years back.

"What do you mean?" she asks, turning back to me.

"I don't know," I say. "I mean, you were young."

She nods, as if this fact, remembering it, comes as something of a surprise to her. She blinks. "I was young," she says.

I get a job working at a B. Dalton bookstore. The manager has to fill out some forms, and when he asks me how long I will be working—for the whole year or just for the summer—I say, "Just for the summer," without thinking, and by the time I realize, he has already written it down and it doesn't seem worth the trouble of making him go back and change it. Still, I go through the rest of the day with the feeling that I've done something wrong. It's the store on Fifth Avenue, and it's not a bad place to work. I am sent to the main floor, to the middle register, where old women come in pairs and shuffle through the Romance section. I eat lunch in a little park a block from the store, where a man-made waterfall keeps tumbling down over itself and secretaries drink diet soda. There is a cool breeze, because of the water. It is the second week of the summer, and on returning from lunch I am told I will have Wednesday off, because it is the Fourth of July.

Riding the bus home, I begin thinking that maybe my mother called my father anyway. It's terrible. The bus keeps stopping, and people keep piling in, and meanwhile I am imagining their conversation going on. If I could make the bus go faster, maybe I could get home in time to stop them. I try to make mental contact with the bus driver by concentrating. I think, Skip the next stop; but he, out of loyalty to the other passengers or simple psychic deafness, doesn't, and instead the bus keeps stopping and people keep getting off and on. Walking into our building, I get the feeling everyone knows. Even the people on the elevator scowl. Maybe if I had told my mother myself, I could have softened it somehow. What would upset her now is not only the money—although the money would be a big part of it—but also that I tried to put something over on her. I am almost afraid to open our door. "Hello," I call, stepping inside.

As it turns out, my mother isn't home. There is a note on the table. She has gone shopping. I look at the note for a while, to see if I can figure anything out from it. For example, it is a short note. Would she usually write a longer one? It isn't signed "Love" or anything—just "Mom," in the scratchy way she draws her pictures.

I hang my jacket in the closet and then turn on my mom's

answering machine. There is one hang-up, and then a message from my father. It makes my whole body go cold. His voice sounds farther away than when we talked the last time. "Richard?" he says. His voice is slow. "This is your father. I just wanted to call to see how things were going. I had an interesting discussion with your mother this afternoon, and we can talk about it later, if you'd like. Call back if you get a chance." Then there is the clatter of his phone being hung up, followed by a little electronic squawk as the connection is broken, which the machine has recorded. I play it again, but there is no way of telling just what he and Mom talked about. I walk into the bathroom and splash cold water on my face and look in the mirror. Then I try reading my mom's note again, but all I can really make it say is that she has gone to the supermarket.

My mother comes home, carrying two big bags of groceries. She pushes the door open with her shoulder. "Can you give me a hand?" she says.

I stand up and take the bags from her and carry them into the kitchen. They are heavy even for me. I hold them close to my chest, where the edges brush against my nose, giving me their heavy, dusty smell. My mom stands in the dining area. She rests one hand on the table. She is wearing running shorts and a T-shirt that on the front says "Perrier" and on the back has the name and date of a race she ran. "Any messages?" she asks me.

I look at her, but I can't tell anything from her face, either. She looks angry, but that could just be because it was hot outside, or because there was too long a line at the supermarket. "I didn't look," I answer. "Don't you even say hello anymore?"

"Hello," she says. She picks up her note and holds it so I can see. "You could throw this away, you know," she says. "Or are you saving it for any particular reason?"

18

"No, you can throw it away."

"That's nice. How about you throw it away?"

"I'm unloading the groceries right now."

She puts the note back down on the table and then walks into the living room. I unload the rest of the groceries. There is a box of spaghetti, Tropicana orange juice, brown rice, pita bread, a few plain Dannon yogurts. I put everything away. and then I fold up the bags and stuff them into the broom closet, where we save them for garbage.

In the living room I hear my mother turn on the machine. There is the hang-up, and then my father's message begins again. "Richard?" he says. "This is your father." I walk into the living room. Mom is standing over the machine, one hand on the buttons. "Oh, God," she says, in a bored way, when she hears his voice, and she shuts it off. Then she turns around and looks at me. I am standing near the wall. "Why do you have that funny look on your face, Richard?" she asks.

I shrug. "How was your day?" I say.

"Bad." She steps over her chair and sits down on the sofa. From the way she arranges herself, I can tell she is upset. She keeps her arms folded across her stomach, and there is something compressed and angry about her face. The way her lips are pressed together—and also something around her eyes. "You want to make me some tea?"

"What happened?" I ask.

"Nothing happened. I ran. I went shopping. I spoke to your father."

I pull a chair over from the table and sit down across from her. I count to five and then ask, "What did he say?"

She shakes her head and laughs through her nose. "Oh, God. He was awful, Richard. Just awful. Right when he got on the phone, he started asking if you'd found a job, and then when I asked him if he was planning to pay the rest of your tuition he laughed and said of course not. He said it was time for you to learn to take care of yourself. He said it was going to be good for you. I couldn't talk to him. Really, Richard, he was awful. I mean it. Just awful."

"I told you not to call him."

"Well, then, I was stupid, Richard."

"Are you going to call him again?"

"How do I know if I'm going to call him again? Not if he keeps acting that way on the phone to me. But I can't pay the school myself." Her lips go back to being tight, and she pulls her arms closer together, so that each hand curls under the opposite elbow.

It occurs to me that what's pressing down on her face is the money we owe the school. "Did the school call again?" I guess.

She nods. "Yesterday."

"Don't call him," I say.

"Thanks, Richard. You want to get me some tea?"

"How about 'please'?"

"How about throwing that note away? Or are you planning to leave it there till Christmas?"

The next day, I get the same feeling that she has called my father again. I go outside during lunch to phone her. It is very hot, and the undersides of my arms are soggy. I have to walk about two blocks down Fifth Avenue before I can find a free phone, and then when I dial our number there is no answer. I think I may have dialed the number wrong, because even if no one is home there should still be the machine, but when I try again there is still no answer. As I hang up, I catch my reflection in the shiny front of the phone for a second and I look awful, sweaty. The rest of the day is terrible. I can hardly work. I keep ringing up the paperbacks as Calendars and the children's books as Software. On the way home, I think that even if my father didn't tell her, I will have to tell her myself. I'm afraid that if I don't something awful will happen, like we'll never speak to each other again or something. But when I get home she is sitting on the sofa, reading the newspaper with her feet up on a chair, and when I walk into the living room she smiles at me, and it just doesn't seem like the right time. I take off my tie and blazer and then pour myself a glass of milk and sit down next to her. She smells like Ben-Gay—a strong, wintergreenish smell—which is what she rubs on her legs after running.

"How was your day?" she asks me. She has a mug of tea on the cushion next to her, and when I sit down she folds up the newspaper and picks up the mug.

"Fine," I say. Then I ask, "Did you go somewhere? I tried calling around noon, but there was no answer."

"I drove up to Greenwich," she says.

"Why didn't you turn on the machine?"

"What are you, the police inspector? I didn't feel like it, that's why."

"But why'd you drive up to Greenwich?"

She laughs. "I feel like I should have one of those big lights on me." She brings her arms in very close to her sides and speaks very quickly, like a suspect: "I don't know. I don't know why I went up to Greenwich." She drinks from her cup, which she holds with both hands. Then she shakes her head and laughs.

We eat dinner. When we lived in Greenwich, she used to teach art in the summers, too. They had a summer day program, with a bunch of little kids running around—I was in it, too, when I was younger—and she used to take them out into the fields and have them draw trees and flowers. She hated it. While we are eating, I get the idea that maybe this is what she went up there for, to talk to someone about this job. Dinner is cool things: tuna fish and pita bread and iced coffee. My mother has a salad. We don't talk for a while. All we do is crunch.

"Why'd you go up to Greenwich?" I ask her again.

She looks up at me, a little angry. The rule, I know, is that we don't talk about anything once she has clearly finished talking about it. "I felt like it," she says. Then she forks some more salad into her mouth and maybe thinks that her response is off key, not really in keeping with the way the apartment feels, because she says, "I had a great idea while I was up there, though."

"What?"

"I thought we could go up tomorrow. You know, for the Fourth of July. See the fireworks. I thought it'd be a lot of fun."

"It sounds great."

"Yes," she says. "I thought you'd like that."

I sleep late the next day, and when I wake up she has gone jogging. She has left me a note saying so, which I throw away. She comes back sweaty and happy, drinking a bottle of club soda, and I ask her why she isn't drinking tea, and we joke, and it all feels very nice, until I remember about Dad and the money and her job and then I feel awful again, because it seems as if all our talking and joking is going on in midair, without anything underneath it to hold it up. We eat lunch, and then my mom makes some sandwiches and we get into our car and drive up the thruway to Connecticut. It's fun seeing the place where you used to live. We drive by our old house, and it looks the same, though there are some toys in the backyard and some lawn furniture—chairs and a big wooden table—which we didn't own. I get this funny feeling while we are in the car that we could still be living inside, as a family; that my father could walk out on the lawn and wave to us, or that if we stayed long enough we might see ourselves going past a window or walking over to sit at that big table. When we get to the high school cars are everywhere, loading and unloading, families carrying big plastic coolers filled with food. I ask my mother if it was always this popular. "Yes," she says. "You just don't remember." We have to drive up the street about two blocks to find a space. By the time we have taken our own cooler out of the trunk, two more cars have already parked in front of us.

The fireworks are always held in the same place. The people sit on the athletic field and the fireworks are set off from behind the baseball diamond, about a hundred yards away. Thousands of people are sitting on blankets or walking around and talking to each other. It's like a scene from one of those movies where the dam bursts and everyone is evacuated to a municipal building, only instead of all their belongings the people here are carrying pillows and Cokes and Twinkies. We find a spot right in the middle of the field. Some kids are playing a game of tag. They keep running through the crowd, laughing, screaming, just barely missing the people on the ground, which of course is part of the fun. When one of the kids brushes against my mother's shoulder I can see that she wants to stop him, give him a talking to, but I ask her not to. I remember when I would have been playing, too.

There is a black platform in the center of the baseball field, and after about three-quarters of an hour a presentation begins. A fireman and a policeman and a man from the Chamber of Commerce walk back and forth to the microphone and give each other awards, for safety and diligence and community service. Then they step down and a group of boys and girls collect onstage, most of them blond, all of them in white robes. The man from the Chamber of Commerce, wearing his silver community service medal, introduces them as the Royal Danish Boys and Girls Choir, "all the way from Holland." Then he leaves the stage, and though I imagine that the children will sing Danish folk songs, or maybe European anthems, what they sing is a medley of Broadway show tunes, in English, designed around the theme of a foreigner's impressions of America: "Oklahoma!" and "Getting to Know You" and "Gary, Indiana," though it is hard to make out the exact words through their accents.

By the time they have finished, the sky has turned dark blue, with the moon hanging just to one side. The policeman and the fireman return with the man from the Chamber of Commerce. "Good evening," he says. His voice echoes all over the field. "We'd like to welcome all of you to this year's celebration of the Greenwich, Connecticut, Fourth of July. In keeping with the spirit of this very special day, we'd like all of you to rise for the singing of our national anthem." My mother and I stand to sing, and there is something nice about being part of this wave of people, of voices. During the last line, there is a popping sound like a champagne bottle opening, and a yellow streak rises over the platform, nosing its way into the sky. The words "and the home, of the, brave" are lost in a chorus of "Oh"s. We sit down again, en masse. I hand my mother her sweater. I can barely see her, but her voice comes from where I know she should be: "Thank you." The fireworks go off over the outfield, sometimes one, sometimes two or three at a time. Each one leaves a little shadow of smoke that the next one, bursting, illuminates. Some bloom like flowers; others are simply midair explosions, flashes. A few burst and then shoot forward, like the effect in *Star Wars* when the ship goes into hyperspace. Some are designed to fool us: one pops open very high in the air, sending out a circle of streamers like the frame of an umbrella; the crowd begins to "Ooh." Then one of these streamers, falling, pops open itself, sending out another series, and the rest of the crowd goes "Ah." Finally, one of these pops open right over our heads, giving off a final shower of color, and the crowd whistles and applauds. The display gets more and more elaborate, until, for the last few minutes, there are ten or twenty rockets in the air at once, bursting and unfolding simultaneously. Everyone starts cheering, and the noises keep booming over us, making us duck our heads. The air smells like sulfur.

In the car, I am close to sleep. My mother is driving, outside it is dark, and I feel safe. The roads are crowded at first, but as we get farther away from the school the traffic gets thinner and thinner, until we are driving alone down mostly empty roads. We seem to drive for a long time before joining up with the main highway, where we become again simply one car among many.

"I'm working this summer," my mother announces, after a little while.

I know, but I ask "Where" anyway.

"Here," she says. "At the school. I got my old job back."

"Mom."

She stops me. "I thought about it, and I decided that it really was important for me to have you in school right now. It was my decision to make, and I made it."

I turn to look at her. Her face is lit up by the dials and meters in the dashboard. It's a surprise to remember that she has a body to go with her voice. I look at her profile, at her cheek and at the skin underneath her chin beginning to sag. I remember how frightened she was when we first moved to the city, how odd it had felt being in a house without my father's voice filling it, and how when we drove up to college for the first time last fall and she saw my name on top of my registration folder she walked out of the reception hall. I found her outside, on the main green, crying. "I can't believe we did it, we pulled it off," she said, meaning college.

"I just don't want to be a burden," I say now.

"You are," she says. "But it's okay. I mean, I'm your mother, and you're supposed to be my burden." She turns to look at me in the dark. "I am your mother, aren't I?"

"As far as I know."

She laughs, and then we don't talk for a while. She turns on the air conditioner. I close my eyes and lean my head against the window. Every so often we hit a bump, which makes the window jiggle, which makes my teeth click together. "I'm sorry you have to work," I say.

"Look, you should be. Don't ask me to get rid of your guilt for you. If you feel guilty, that's fine. This was just important to me, that's all."

Her using the word "guilt" frightens me. I sit up and open my eyes. "What did Dad say to you on the phone?" I ask.

"Nothing. He said he wasn't going to pay for you. He said he was doing the right thing. He said you understood. Do you?"

"No."

She nods, driving. "That's what I told your father. He said you should call him, if you want to. Do you?"

I laugh. "No."

She nods again. "I told him that, too."

She seems ready to stop talking, but I keep going. I want her to tell me that it's okay, that she missed working outdoors, that she missed the little kids, missed Connecticut. "I just feel bad because now you can't go to Wellfleet for the summer."

My mother says, "Let's not talk."   ·

We drive. Through the windshield everything looks purple and slick—the road and the taillights of the cars passing us and the slender, long-necked lights hanging over the highway. We seem sealed in, as if we are traveling underwater.

My mother reaches over and turns off the air conditioner. "There is something I want to talk to you about, Richard," she says.

"What?" I ask.

She keeps her face turned toward the highway. "If anything like this ever happens again, I want you to tell me immediately. Don't make it so I have to find out myself. This whole thing wouldn't have happened if you had told me about it in the spring. We could have gotten loans and things. As it is now, we're stuck."

I don't say anything.

"If you ever have anything to tell me," she says, "tell me when it happens, okay? We're very close. You can tell me anything you want to. Okay?"

She looks over at me. I try to keep my face from showing anything, and when I can't do that I look away, at my feet under the dashboard. It is an offer. I can tell her or not. The funny thing is, I can feel that she doesn't really want me to. If she has guessed, she doesn't want me to confirm it. And though I am relieved, it seems to me that if I don't tell her now I never will, and this thing will always be between us, this failure, my father's voice embedded in static.

I look up. My mother is waiting for me, we are passing under the George Washington Bridge.

"Okay," I say.

LIGHTS

I NEVER LOVED Susan Fllis. I fell into our affair through a friend of hers. I loved the friend. I went to spend time at the friend's house and Susan—her housemate—was always there. She was a small, dark-haired girl, very well dressed (in that prep school, ski team way, dark red sweaters and Bean boots; later, I did find out she'd been on the ski team). It irritated me that she seemed to have no idea she was disturbing us. There I'd be, feeling that excited sensation I get whenever I'm trying to be charming (a slight rising in the chest and lower throat, like watching someone else do something risky, like tightrope walking), and this other girl would sit down, cross-legged, and begin contributing to our discussion. Right from the start I saw her as a slowing, dulling influence. The quick, cutting conversations I had with Judy were impossible with Susan around. Judy was a taller, slimmer, more intelligent girl from New York, which is where I'm from too. She had an attractively long nose—forward and then down, like a flattened VW bug. But she was very attractive, as I said, and when I made a joke, an illicit joke, she would catch the front of her tongue with her teeth, as if to show she was physically hampering herself

31

from fully enjoying my humor. Our conversations had the hidden chargedness all conversations between New Yorkers of the opposite sex have, that suppressed energy you otherwise find only in taxicabs, where everyone talking is pretending not to be watching the meter. But Susan would thump downstairs, come into the living room, see me there, and flop down on the couch beside Judy. "Oh, hi," she'd say, with a smile. "We're talking about *Issues*," Judy would explain, which was the name of the more controversial publication on campus but which would have described our other conversations as well. The light would go out of Judy's face (her eyes had an intricate way of folding and crinkling when she bit her tongue, something she never did when Susan was around), and I would feel the lightness in my throat and chest sinking downward. It would become instead a kind of leadenness in my stomach.

Towards the end of my courting of Judy, we went to a reading together. Let me just pause here to explain what I mean by "courting." My courtships generally take too long. I courted Judy for about a month, but we never actually went out to dinner formally or met anywhere for drinks. I was trying to sound her out—in my relations with women, I am essentially like a cautious bank, feeling out a company for a possible takeover bid. I'd be out jogging and "stop by" Judy's house, which was down the street from my dorm and thus made for a good excuse. This became the point of my jogging. I'd pick out good ensembles, then run until sweat was pouring down my face before panting my way over (the wolfman pursuing his prey) to Judy's door. A girl I'd liked in high school had once told me that she couldn't imagine me doing anything physical. Since then, I've always made it a point for women I'm interested in to see this side of me, the sweaty, exhausted side. It's a preview, I suppose, of what I'll look like after sex. Anyway, my courtship consisted mainly of these toweling-downs in Judy's living room (while cringing at the sound of feet on the stairs), and also of meeting Judy around campus and telling her stories about mutual friends which would make her bite her tongue.

When she invited me to the reading—Grace Paley, at the Methodist church downtown—I felt I'd finally reached the point I wanted to be at with her. I dressed very carefully in my room, then walked over to her house. But the reading turned out to be a disaster, and the end of our non-affair. We went with two of her housemates—Fred and Rob—and also another boy. This other was dark, and riveting. I knew immediately why he was there, standing around in the living room while we all waited for Judy. His skin was oliveish in color, his hair—while mine was always carefully short—was shaggy. And where I had to dress carefully, his clothes, dark, rumpled, seemed to have simply fallen on him correctly, or to have been generated from inside him, like a leopard's spots or a caterpillar's bumpy skin. "Daniel?" Fred said. "Have you met Jimmy Osteroz?" I hadn't; we shook hands. I gave him a burning look, but he retained his soft, at-home composure. I could see that he had the sort of liquid, magnetic quality that attracted girls like Judy—like a phosphorescent fish down in the lower parts of the ocean, drawing all the light-seeking plankton to him. Jimmy—even above sea level—was blazing. I fell into a gloomy mood. Judy came plunking downstairs next to Susan. Susan wasn't coming with us to the reading; she was just going to the kitchen. As Judy went to Jimmy—no jokes or pithy comments, he just walked over to her and kissed her lightly on the cheek—I went, with relief, to Susan. This was to be our pattern. She looked up at me (I was much taller than she) with a kind of agitated happiness, her head going back and forth like a cat's, trying to take all of me in. "I didn't know Judy knew Judd Nelson," I said, tilting towards Jimmy. Susan's face clouded for a moment; she wasn't sure I was joking. Then she laughed and said, "Haven't you met Jimmy Osteroz?" She was trying to feel her way out over the conversational terrain she felt Judy and I explored in our discussions. "This is a big night. Judy's had a crush on him for a year. This is the first time he's ever taken her anyplace."

Well, it's clear how that went. Jimmy Osteroz was the kind of man I've always lost the women I liked to. For whereas he, and those like him, are real leopards, or true caterpillars, I am like some other animal, miming their spots and skin textures in order to escape detection and steal food. The Paley reading was a bore, and now that it's two years ago I can barely remember it. All I can remember is sitting uncomfortably in the pew next to Judy, with Fred and Rob to my right and Jimmy to her left. I was burning the entire night. Paley, a small woman with wild hair and high-top basketball shoes, rose to the podium and made a brief, semi-inflammatory speech about women in America, on the theme that we all, apparently, still had a long way to go. The people in the packed church politely clapped. Paley's voice, as I recall, was rich, but for the life of me I can't remember a thing she read. I was too busy watching Judy in her natural element, whispering small remarks into Jimmy's ear, making him smile. I was conscious of our legs touching in the crowded pew, but it clearly meant nothing—on the other side, my legs were also touching Fred Horowitz's.

I was later to learn more about both Jimmy and Judy; Jimmy was Venezuelan, and had originally been in the class of 1983. It ended up taking him seven years to graduate. He was from a wealthy family, and had drug problems. Throughout the winter and spring—until, with

equal relief, both Judy and the school said good-bye to him
forever—he would torment Judy with alternating bouts of
cruelty and indifference. For weeks at a time, Judy would
retire to her room, sleeping and not coming out. Susan
would report that some mornings she found her vomiting
in the bathroom (like most intelligent women, Judy had at
one time in her life had an eating disorder). But the affair,
on the other hand, seemed to please Judy, to feed some
appetite she had for tragic glamour, to play into the image
she had of herself as a sophisticated girl who was playing
her life, even at this young age, perhaps a little too hard.
There were many problems associated with being our age,
and Judy wasn't going to miss out on any of them. How I
envied Jimmy! And though I would come to think that
perhaps Judy would have been a bad choice for me, I
would sometimes wonder what it would have changed to
have had her, to have spent a year suffering with her and
soothing her. She was the closest, Judy Berman of East
20th Street, Manhattan, I ever came to dating the sorts of
girls I've never dated. Who knows how finally crossing that
hurdle would have altered me?

Anyway, exit Judy and Jimmy. The night after the reading, I came home to find a message on my machine. It was
from Susan. "Daniel?" she said. "It's, ah, Susan Ellis. I have
tickets to the Renoir show in Boston, for Wednesday, and I
was wondering if you'd like to come." She left her number—
the same number, of course, as Judy's. My first response was
anger. The only way she could have gotten my number was
from Judy. I felt like a ballplayer, and that these two girls
had met, hammered out a deal, and I had been traded to the
less desirable team. Judy—and Susan, too, because she'd sat
in on our post-jogging discussions—knew I was an art
history major, and that I was interested in museums and

shows. The whole thing was somehow humiliating, and I decided not to call Susan Ellis back.

Let's discuss here, too, the common wisdom that you don't get women if you too-clearly want them. Obviously, it's not completely true (Jimmy clearly "wanted" Judy, just as Judy clearly wanted Jimmy), but it is partially true. Perhaps what's more accurate is that some girls respond best to distance, that a true coldness excites them more than emotion. For I'd never been at all warm to Susan Ellis; I'd say brief, cutting things to her and then continue my discussions with Judy. (We'd be talking about names; I'd say I didn't like mine—Daniel Julian—Judy would say she'd always liked hers, and then Susan would chime in, from her cross-legged position on the couch, that she didn't like hers either. Me: "Well of course not. It's like the name of a fictitious magazine reporter on *Days of Our Lives*.") Plus, it does seem like fate, if random, is still somehow patterned, like crystal. I'd fallen onto a track which led straight to Susan. On the way to class, walking my usual route, I saw her walking a block or so ahead of me. I turned up a different street. But then later, walking towards the post office, I heard her voice behind me: "Daniel? Hi." I turned around, and Susan Ellis jogged a little to catch up. She was squinting. "Did you get the message I called yesterday?"

"Sure. It was on my machine."

"So do you want to come at all? The reason I'm asking is that it's this Wednesday, and if you don't want to go I should probably find someone else to use the ticket. Judy was going to, but she's going to dinner with Judd Nelson instead." She looked at me, trying this out, seeing how I'd react.

"It's fine," I said. "I'd like to go."

Wednesday night, she came to pick me up at my dorm. I walked out and got into the car with her. It was a purple

Volvo station wagon—Fred Horowitz's, it turned out. I said it was nice, and Susan said, "You like it? Fred's trying to sell it. He offered it to me, but I said I didn't really need a car. Do you want to buy it?"

"No, no; I just meant I've always liked Volvos." The ultimate joke, it seemed to me, would be to end up not only without Judy, but also owning Fred Horowitz's car. Still, it was a fine evening. The little warm space of the Volvo made us intimate. It occurred to me early on that I'd either have to be charming or else we'd both be bored, so I made jokes all night. I liked Susan because she laughed easily. Not uncritically, but when I made a good joke she'd reward it accordingly, with a full smile, not with the tongue-biting Judy had granted. It was a pleasant drive, with the road around us all purple and liquid and the other cars, with their myriad signals and shiftings, silently gliding by. Night driving always makes me feel connected to the other drivers, as if we're all part of one great nocturnal migration. The Boston Museum was lit up as if for a premiere: it felt dashing walking in, well dressed, with a pretty girl on my arm. I held Susan's hand as we went through the exhibit. I've always hated Renoir, actually. But the show itself was a good deal of fun. Most of the people were wearing those headsets people wear at shows—ten years behind the technological times—which give you the illusion of walking through the gallery with a really intelligent person by your side. Sound leaked from these headphones, so that it felt as if Susan and I were surrounded by a huge, whispering conspiracy. There were marks on the walls indicating which paintings were on the tape's circuit, and these areas were the most heavily congested, with people flicking their machines on and off in front of them, their buttons making noises like popcorn banging in a pot. I offered these things to Susan—young, well-dressed Susan, whose warm hand was curled up in my own like a letter I was delivering—and she laughed. We walked on past the last nudes, the fat rolling around them in layers, like Hula-Hoops. "They're like the Michelin tire family," I said; Susan laughed. So what I loved in Susan was not her but the success I had with her. I loved the feeling of being charming, of balancing on that high wire over boringness and boisterousness.

I began a courtship of her, five weeks of late-night jogging and dinners out, before finally I kissed her. Judy was sometimes in the house when I came sweating over, and I would feel the slight flutter in my throat, only my attention was directed away from her, towards her smaller, darker housemate. We slept together, finally, in December. When Judy and Jimmy broke up in May, it felt as if with the superior health of our relationship Susan and I were somehow showing her up. Judy's next boyfriend came from the opposite end of the spectrum, a tall, red-haired business major who took Judy to brunch and lacrosse games and lent her books on investment strategies for the nineties. Judy began previewing the problems of the next phase of life: cocktail parties, job politics, sudden downturns in the market. I wondered if anyone ever really dated the people they were suited for, if suitability was even what attracted. For it occurred to me that for Susan, dating me was like my dating Judy Berman: a risk, an accomplishment. And would my own life have been different, somehow, if I'd spent with Judy the two years I spent with Susan? Would there be layers of experiential fat (the rings on a redwood tree) gained or altered? I'd be, in this bag of my skin, different, a different person. We evolve our personalities—as our bodies evolved—in response to stimuli from our immediate surroundings. With a different environment, would I be a new species of Daniel Julian? My feelings about love, certainly, would be different. For love seems to me now less about emotions than about signals, conscious and unconscious, a response not so much to people as to beacons, tugging you in, warning you away, blinkers, turn signals, headlights flashing in the underwater dark.

"SHH"

FOR THE FIRST FEW MINUTES after he arrives at Gregor Krumlich Gallery, Richard, late, can't even find his mother. So many people are here for the opening. A few heads turn when he enters, but seeing it's no one important—just a teenage boy in an orange down jacket—they go back to their conversations again. Richard blushes angrily. He's only here because his mother asked him, he wants to say, and now where is his mother? He walks past the guest book. Everyone is standing with their coats folded over their arms, holding plastic glasses of wine, so Richard's first move—after removing his puffy coat and folding it over his arm with the zipper side showing, hiding the dark round stain on the back—is to head for the drinks table.

Fresh from the table, pushing his hair back with his free hand, he finds his mother in the fifth room he examines. "Richard!" she says. She's talking to Hiroshi, the thin, thick-haired Japanese artist she usually talks to at openings. Richard's mother needs people to speak with—in the same way, Richard thinks, that he needs his folded-over coat and wineglass, in order to be invisible—and, because his accent is so heavy, Hiroshi is always a safe bet. Even at his own openings, nobody ever talks to Hiroshi.

"How you, Richard?" he asks, in his excited way. He's wearing a denim shirt and black Buddy Holly glasses, which he pushes up on his nose.

"Fine, Hiroshi. What about you?" Richard turns to say something to his mother, but she—changing position so as to be standing beside him—taps his forearm, meaning he's being rude and should listen to Hiroshi.

Hiroshi inclines his head, an abbreviated version of the bow he still hasn't completely unlearned from the Royal Academy of Fine Arts in Tokyo. "Fine. Thank you." He gestures with his head at the paintings around them, an S-shaped motion like a trout swimming upstream. "What do you think of the show?"

"It seems okay," Richard says. "What do you think, Hiroshi?"

Hiroshi nods rapidly. "I think it's great, great. Such bold *color*."

Richard's mother, her hand still on his forearm, says, "I was just telling Hiroshi I haven't seen Henry's work since 1984. These new ones are quite a change." Richard nods blankly. He hasn't really looked yet, the paintings have been like the blank faces in a baseball stadium, blurred rectangular witnesses to his search for his mother. He tries to tell from her tone whether she's upset with him for being late, then decides she's not. Once, when he was forty-five minutes late meeting her at the Metropolitan Museum, he couldn't find her at all. He went through the entire André Meyer wing, alone, expecting to see her around every corner, admiring a Pissarro or a Cézanne. When he couldn't turn her up, he went downstairs to the information desk and asked whether a tall, brown-haired woman had left any message. To his

44

surprise, the man there handed him a note, in his mother's handwriting, saying she'd been tired of waiting and had gone home.

Hiroshi, meanwhile, is nodding again. "True. This work is departure."

As if this phrase signals the end of their own conversation, Hiroshi makes another stifled bow—flashing the uncombed top of his head—holds up a little farewell finger, and moves away from them. Richard has learned that there are two kinds of good-byes at openings. There is the friendly kind— like Hiroshi's—which promises that the departing person will be back later, to get your final views on the event (though this rarely actually happens), and then there is the unfriendly kind, which says that the departing person is surprised you came up to speak with him, unhappy that you're in the same social circle, and is resigned to seeing you either at the next such gathering or—preferably—never. Richard walks with his mother back to the entrance of the gallery. She's wearing her dark green Banana Republic skirt, which makes her look a little like Meryl Streep, and a blue crewneck sweater. If Richard had been home, he would have advised against the sweater. He looks at her face anxiously (the features his own, blurred by age and gender), to see if she's wearing too much makeup. When his parents were married, Richard's father would go with his mother to openings; for the past three years, since his freshman year in high school, Richard has gone. What he has learned is that in life, as on the tests he takes in school, neatness counts; everything counts. Often at these events, he feels less like a son than like a wardrobe consultant, one of those men who supervises interactions between the president and the press or public.

His mother is looking at him with raised eyebrows,

knowing she's being inspected. Richard nods, meaning she passes.

She leans closer to him. "Should I talk to Gregor?" she asks.

"Let's wait," he says. "Till the crowd thins out more first."

Richard's mother nods. "You look so grown-up," she says. Then, as if this thought has led her backwards, she gestures at the guest book on the counter next to them. "Did you sign in yet?" she asks. When he was a boy, bored at these openings, Richard would spend his time signing names like "R. Nixon," or "M. T-Tung," hoping to fool artists into thinking important celebrities had been at their shows and they had missed them. Once, he signed in the names of President Carter's entire cabinet, having just that afternoon learned them at school.

Now he signs his own name, Richard Freely, looking first for his mother's name, a page back, the names between marking just how many minutes he is late. "Sorry I'm late," he says.

His mother takes a sip of wine, her swallow becoming the "N" of "No, that's fine. Just as long as you're here now."

She takes the glass away from her lips. It's empty. She looks off towards the drinks table. Separating her from it are people—Henry Atski, the artist whose show this is; Gregor Krumlich himself—Richard knows she isn't ready to speak to yet. Going there now would be like walking across a minefield, each person, each conversational misstep, a potential explosion. Richard takes his mother's glass from her hand (the fingers leave foggy prints) and pours in half the contents of his own. The liquid makes a tiny curved ghost against the inside of the glass as it recedes.

"Thank you," his mother says.

"I only gave you half," he tells her. "I need the rest myself, for a prop."

*   *   *

Richard was supposed to go straight from school to the gallery. He'd hung around the school library till five-thirty, reading. He was trying to kill time, but after two hours of *Time* and *Newsweek* he forgot exactly why and, in his newsprint-induced daze, took the subway home instead. When he got home he was surprised that his mother wasn't there. When she went out, she usually left a Post-it note on the black apartment door (he could thus tell from the elevator, a full thirty feet away, those evenings when he would have to eat dinner alone), and the lack of one surprised him, too. If she were late, there would have been a message on the answering machine (the loud, staticky rumble of a subway in the background). But there was nothing, just her makeup kit open on the sink in front of the mirror and the bathroom light flatly on. Richard put the kit back in its accustomed place on top of the toilet tank, shut off the light, looked at the canvas on the floor of the living room, then went into the kitchen, prepared a plate of peanut butter and Stoned Wheat Thins, and sat in his room eating and watching the news. The news answered all the questions (would there be renewed fighting in the Middle East? Yes) *Time* magazine had just finished asking. It was a quarter to seven, the November light already dying behind the New Jersey apartment complexes across the river, when his mother called.

"Mom," he said, "where are you?"

"Where am I? I'm at Krumlich Gallery. Where are you?" She sounded annoyed, and Richard, his stomach sinking, realized that this answered the other question from the library, which was, Why am I still here so long after school?

"I'm sorry. Jesus, I forgot."

"You must really be blocking," his mother said, and her voice relaxed. She always felt better about his bad behavior

47

when she was able to convert it into psychological terms. "I'll be right over," he said. On the M5 bus going downtown, Broadway liquid and ablaze with streetlights, sleek taxicabs, and lighted storefronts (the mannequins in their habitats as interesting and poignant as the posed animals in the Museum of Natural History), Richard realized she was right. He had been blocking. He hated openings. They all reminded him of *My Fair Lady*, of the scene where Audrey Hepburn makes her debut in society—everyone gets into a long line, and the duchess comes up in that cold, stately procession, takes Audrey's cheeks between her fingertips, tilts her face up, and pronounces, "Charming, charming." Openings were composed of just these moments of brittle, stylized acceptance or rejection. Richard hated Gregor Krumlich openings most of all. His mother was a painter; she had shown at Krumlich five times during the seventies. When her paintings stopped selling, Gregor had asked her, in his cautious, reserved way (as if any communication with the world were an imposition that could be faced only through politely gritted teeth) whether perhaps her work wouldn't show "to better advantage" in another gallery. In the seven years since, his mother still hadn't been able to find one. It was awful for Richard to see her looking at Gregor now. The expression that came over her face during their meetings—proud, envious, hopeful, resentful— was difficult for Richard to characterize, and impossible for him to observe.

Four weeks before, Richard's mother had sent Gregor slides of her newest work. She hadn't heard anything yet, and Richard knew she'd gone to the opening tonight to find out what he thought of the paintings. More than that, Richard knew, she was secretly hoping Gregor would take her back. "It's crazy, right?" she'd said, and Richard had said, "It's not crazy." She blamed Gregor for her not being able to find a gallery; once you've been dropped by the best space in the city, who was going to support you then? Stepping off the elevator, walking towards the gallery, Richard was hit with a sudden picture—his mother sitting alone in a coffee shop, looking at her watch, worrying about her slides in Gregor's office, worrying about whether Richard was going to show up or whether she was going to have to face this opening on her own. The image squeezed Richard's stomach so hard that for a moment he had to stop to catch his breath.

Now, walking next to her, Richard is relieved. She seems to be in a good mood. Krumlich Gallery is arranged like a large plus sign, with a series of side rooms forming the crossbar off a main viewing area. Gregor and Henry Atski are in this main space, so Richard leads his mother through the side rooms. Over his shoulder, he looks in to see what they are doing. Gregor and Henry are standing together in the room's center. There is an informal line of affluent-looking people—potential buyers—waiting to shake hands and exchange greetings or congratulations. Each time one of them steps up, Henry lowers his head a little, smiling warmly in appreciation of a compliment or lifting his eyebrows as reaction to a joke. Henry is the most successful of the painters in Richard's mother's crowd (though there was a nasty rumor two years ago that he had to sell one of his Hofmanns to pay for a new boat). Since moving to Key West, he has perfected his outfit. He's wearing a blue blazer with a bleached white yachting cap, and has a short, neatly cut beard. Hemingwayski, Richard's mother calls him. After shaking hands with Henry, the collectors turn and shake hands with Gregor, who lowers his head with a tight smile, gesturing with his free hand towards the drinks table, sometimes patting an especially dependable collector on the back. The two move with assembly-line efficiency, a department store Santa and his floor manager, competently working a holiday crowd.

In the first room, Richard and his mother run into Lars Stevenson, a burly sculptor. Lars kisses Richard's mother on the cheek, and shakes hands with Richard. His hand, curling around Richard's own, has that special graininess sculptors' hands get, as if they have somehow acquired extra lines in their palms. "How's it going?" he asks, putting those hands into his pockets.

Richard knows he means this just as a commonplace, and he hopes his mother won't answer truthfully, so he cringes a little when she says, "So-so."

"I know what you mean," Lars says quickly, deliberately not pursuing this. "It's been a shit fall." He looks over their shoulders, says, "Excuse me, I haven't said hello to Henry yet. It's a great show, no? I'll talk to you later." Then he kisses Richard's mother on the cheek and walks into the next room. Richard has known Lars since he was seven years old. Two summers in a row, when his mother's popularity was at its peak, she traded paintings for summers at a small house in Southampton between the ocean and the bay. Both times Lars came up, staying for weeks in the spare bedroom. Richard liked him. They had pinecone fights together, and when Lars used the second-floor bathroom he would squirt down out the window at Richard with the green water pistol he kept on the radiator. Now, Lars has a kind of nervousness around Richard's mother, as if he's afraid she's going to remind him of this friendship in order to unfairly get something out of it.

To cover both their disappointments, his mother says,

"You haven't said what you think of Henry's pictures yet."

Richard looks. The paintings are all blue, all around eight feet tall. "They look like the monolith in *2001*," Richard says. His mother laughs. He knows that one of his unspoken jobs here is to keep his mother relaxed, laughing.

"Try to really look, though," she says.

"I *am* looking," Richard says. But what he is looking for, in the craggy surfaces of the paintings, is the foothold of a joke, the crevice of a comic idea he can latch on to. The pictures have been done with acrylic gel. The artist swabs a quick-drying, colorless goo onto the canvas, for texture, then paints over it. The finished product attains a mountains-and-valleys effect, like a relief map. "They look like garbage bags left overnight in the rain," Richard tries. This only makes his mother smile, so he looks for something else, at the list of prices and titles in his hand. He feels a brightening in his head. "And these titles: *Putting On His Knowledge* and *Transfigured Gaiety*. What's the point? He should just call them by their prices. *Fourteen Thousand Seven Hundred* or *Twenty Thousand Dollars*."

"They're quotes from Yeats," his mother says, sobering.

Richard is going to say something else, but he realizes his mother isn't listening. She's altered her face into an intelligent, attentive expression. Richard doesn't understand why, and then he looks up and sees a woman he recognizes coming towards them. It's Lara Silverstein, the art critic. She has a long, tubular nose and squinted eyes, as if she's trying to physically edit the crowd down to just those people she wants to see. "Hi, Lara," Richard's mother says, as they pass. Lara says, "Joan," flatly. It is a neutral fact—his mother's name—and not a greeting. Richard's mother's face relaxes.

"That was Lara Silverstein," she whispers.

"I know who it was," Richard says.

"That bitch," his mother says, taking another sip of wine. In the next room are a number of people Richard knows, standing in small clumps, drinking and socializing. Herbert Tingly is in the corner, talking to his wife and a woman Richard doesn't recognize. Herbert—who likes to gesture as he speaks—is revolving his cigarette-holding hand so vigorously that he seems to be trying to make a lariat with the smoke. He and Richard's mother lock eyes for a moment, then both turn away. Years ago, Richard knows, Herbert suggested that he and Richard's mother sleep together. Richard's mom asked if they couldn't just stay friends. In response, Herbert hasn't spoken to her since 1979. "I guess that meant no," is how his mother sums up the story.

Past Herbert is thin Ken Worthy, another art critic. He's in the middle of a conversation with two painters and a doughy couple, collectors. Richard follows his mother over to them. They stand next to Ken until he finishes what he's saying. Ken used to be director of the contemporary wing of the Baltimore Museum, but when one of the trustees wanted to donate a David Salle, he had quit rather than accepting it. This act has made him a kind of saint in this circle. Everyone does him favors. One afternoon, when Richard came home from school, Ken and his wife were asleep on the futon in the living room. They'd just gotten in from Europe, and Richard's mother had lent them the apartment for a nap before the long drive back to their house in Connecticut. "Shh," the Post-it note on the door had said, though Richard had not understood it until stepping into the dim, night-smelling living room, the sleeping figures lying clasped with a kind of lost intensity like the figures in a Rossetti drawing.

"Hi, Joan," Ken says, angling his head towards her. The

doughy couple, seeing this is someone Ken knows, smile in neutral unison.

"Hi," Richard's mother says. "What've you been up to?"

"Visiting different studios, poking around. What about you?"

"I've been painting," Richard's mother says, and Ken's face undergoes a quick change, as if by mentioning her own work Richard's mother has violated an unspoken rule between them.

"That's great," Ken says, making to turn back to his conversation.

"You should come by and see the work while you're in the city," Richard's mother says.

"That would be great," Ken says. He takes her hand. "Listen, why don't I give you a call before the end of the week. All right?" They kiss.

Richard's mother nods. "So I'll talk to you Thursday?" she says, and Richard steps on her foot. Ken nods.

After they've moved away, before Richard can say anything, his mother says, "I know. That wasn't too bright, right?"

"Right," he says.

"Well, fuck it, what am I supposed to do? Pretend I'm not a painter?"

"No," Richard says. "But I don't see why I have to come to these things if you're not even going to listen to what I say."

Richard's mother laughs. "It can't be any worse than when I go to school for parent-teacher night. It's always so heartbreaking. I go in there with all the other parents, everyone looking serious and dressed up. We all sit at our desks, waiting our turns. Every other mother goes up, gives her name, and then the teacher says, 'Oh yes, Alicia is such a joy to have in class.' I go up, say who I am, and they take my wrist and say, 'You're Richard *Freely's* mother?' and then they spend the next half hour telling me how you act out in class. Think of this as a trade-off.''

They come around the next corner, and there's Tom Dancer. Tom works in art law—he has neither the secure look of the collectors (staring out from a kind of tinted windshield of money), nor the edginess of the artists—and, Richard thinks, he has always had a crush on his mother. He excuses himself from the people he's with and comes right over and starts talking, adjusting the tilt of his glasses as if fine-tuning a thought. He gossips to Richard's mother about the other people here, making her laugh. Richard stands next to her, feeling relieved to have found somebody else for his mother to talk to, but at the same time vaguely rejected, usurped. Plus, he can't think of a subtle way to leave, without making it clear what he was doing here in the first place. As Tom talks, Richard's mother raises her glass to her lips and carefully finishes off her wine. Then she lowers her arm and taps the back of Richard's hand with the flexible, faintly moist surface of the plastic. "Excuse me for a second, Tom," she says. "Richard, could you get me another glass of wine, please?" They've gone to so many openings together, she's got these signals down pat.

It is only at these sorts of times that Richard envies his older brother, who lives with their father in Los Angeles. At first, Richard's father had said he didn't want to "break the boys up," as if Richard and his brother were a pair of Queen Anne chairs that looked particularly good together. After the divorce went through, though, and it became clear that Richard's father wasn't going to get custody of both of them, he had asked if either child wanted to come to California.

Richard's brother had elected to go. Richard has visited Los Angeles a number of times. Richard's father handles advertising for a company that imports European sports cars, and the only tense moments in the house are when his commercials appear on television. They're always the same. A car drives much too quickly down a winding mountain road. It brakes, accelerates, runs through puddles. After it's over, their father always turns to them with the same tense, worried expression and asks, "Well, how about it kids, huh? Does it make you want to buy the product?" Even when they were ten and eleven, Richard and his brother had always assured him that yes, if they were in the market for a German luxury sedan, their first choice would be an Audi.

Walking through the gallery alone, Richard tries to clarify his feelings. He's not so much angry at his mother for bringing him here as he is at the people here for treating her the way they do. What Richard has always wanted to do is make some sort of grand gesture, say, "What, it's okay to sleep at our house, Ken, but you can't even put my mother in a single group show, huh?" But he knows this wouldn't help anything. These people simply will not be nice to his mother until she starts doing well, and she can't do well until they start being nice to her. There is really nothing Richard can do to help her. This is what helplessness actually feels like.

He looks at Gregor, standing next to Henry, looking over the tops of the collectors' heads, counting how many are left. Richard is sure Gregor has seen his mother, and if he hasn't gone over to talk to her on his own, the news can't be good. The thing is, once Gregor makes up his mind about something, he stays set. Richard remembers how, on his mother's thirty-sixth birthday, the year she sold sixty paintings, she threw a huge party at her studio. This is the image that comes to Richard's mind most frequently when he tries to remember her as a success. She was wildly excited. It was exhausting watching his mother move among these people, like watching a relative on a tightrope. Richard had gone into her room, just to sit down and get his bearings. There was Gregor Krumlich, on the telephone, in a double-breasted suit. He was speaking intently, and when Richard entered he looked up for the briefest moment. "I'm Richard Freely," Richard said. Gregor nodded, said hello, then went back to his conversation. It had struck Richard then—the unfairness of it—that there was nothing he could do to particularize himself for this man, nothing he could do that would ever make him live in his eyes as anything more than Joan Freely's son. Richard would do anything to keep his mother from having her conversation with Gregor now. He knows what will happen. She'll be depressed for a few weeks or so. Then, after a month, she'll begin painting again, with someone new in mind to show the work to. But how long can this go on? Richard has always hoped, secretly, that she would have a gallery by now. Otherwise, when he goes to college next September, who will take her to openings? What if Hiroshi takes English lessons, or Tom Dancer develops a crush on someone else? Who will his mother talk to then?

Hiroshi is across the room from Richard, holding his wineglass with both hands out, like a rugby player with a football. Richard feels with his pinky for the little sharp plastic nipple at the bottom of his own glass, enjoying the slight pain. Hiroshi nods and smiles. Before Richard can walk over to him, his mother is by his side. He feels her first as a sort of warmth to his left. "Whew," she says. "That was long."

"How's Tom?" Richard asks.

"Fine. We're old friends, you know." The crowd around Atski and Krumlich is breaking up. Krumlich is patting people on the back, working his way towards his office. Richard's mom takes a deep breath, says, "Wish me luck," and leaves her wineglass in Richard's hand. Her departure seems to make a faint ghost in the air. She walks jauntily towards Gregor Krumlich, and Richard is glad that, from this angle, whatever her face is doing, he doesn't have to see it. She says, "Gregor!" in a warm voice. Gregor turns to see who it is. When he sees it's Richard's mother, he says, "Hello, Joan," in his accented English and moves to talk to someone else. This is the second kind of good-bye. But Richard's mother keeps walking towards him, so Gregor— with a small, resigned expression, as if the effort of being visibly rude is just too great—has to turn back, to face her again.

Half an hour later, Richard is in a cab going home. His mother has gone to the post-opening party downtown. In the hallway, before splitting up, Richard asked, "How'd it go?" and his mother, now holding the envelope she'd mailed to Gregor a month ago, had sourly shrugged: "Okay; there's a note inside." In the cab, bouncing towards the 66th Street transverse, Richard opens the envelope and takes out the plastic transparency sheet, the slides all in their little square see-through holders. Clipped to the upper edge is a brief note, on Krumlich Gallery stationery: "Joan—Thanks for sharing these with me." It accounts for his mother's sardonic expression at the door. Richard wants to crumple this note up, tear it into shreds and throw them out the window, but instead he detaches it from the sheet and slides it carefully back into the envelope. Then he holds the slide sheet against the taxi window and looks, with the bouncing, shifting light of the street lamps, at the paintings Krumlich doesn't care about. Still lifes: high-key colored canvases of chairs, cups, saucers, fruits; the objects, the talismans, of his sliding daily life.

NEAR EDGARTOWN

WE WENT FOR A ride that evening, Jonathan, Eric, and I. Matthew, sulking over his sunburned skin, did not come along. I stood at the edge of his bed—addressing his knees, for he sat on the topmost bunk—and asked as nicely as I could, but he said he preferred to stay behind. He was angry with us. He'd fallen asleep, unlotioned, on the beach, and we had let him doze; he blamed us for his burn. As I turned he flicked on his tape recorder. Haydn rose from his bedside. He played classical music at high volume, hoping that someone would notice and ask him to lower it. Then he could say, "You mean, you don't like late baroque music?" He was the sort of unhandsome, serious boy for whom culture was like an expensive car; he was always willing to show it off.

In the kitchen of the hostel Eric stood by a counter with Emily, going over a shopping list. Someone rapped the window behind me. I turned, and Jon was standing outside, smiling, his biking gloves on, his helmet hanging jauntily by its straps from his belt. The paraphernalia, I assume, made him feel more serious, for he would not ride without it. He mouthed the words "come on" and pointed at the sky, which was clouding. It was nearly six. The other groups at the hostel were eating already, chewing with their mouths open, talking and joking and making with their combined voices a kind of deep beehive sound. Most of the boys, the thinner ones, did not wear shirts. Their shoulders were dabbed with red, marking where the sun, sneakily, had painted their backs as they rode. Unlike Matthew, they carried these burns as trophies. Eric's hair was sandy-colored. It was long, and dripped over his ears and forehead in tiny curls. Emily was our group leader. She was barely nineteen but had, in the confusion of her eyes, a look which seemed to have come from experience. During the ferry rides which carried us from island to island—we were on a two-week bike trip—as Eric and Matthew and Jon and I stood by the railing, looking over to watch the water slapping against the sides of the boat, she and the girls would form tight circles where she would describe for them her sexual encounters. Once, one of the girls came over to where Jon and I were standing and asked, in a distressed voice, if it was true, if men really did prefer oral sex to intercourse. The question seemed more intended for me than for Jon. Jon was very much a virgin, short and a little wide around the upper hips. Still, he answered before I could, joked bravely, "We like nasal sex best." The girl didn't see the joke in this, though Jon and I laughed. She was from the suburb of a suburban city, and did not understand much.

Emily gave us directions to the supermarket and Eric the money for our shopping. We walked down the hall to the door, our backpacks empty weights across our shoulders. Jon was waiting outside, standing with his bike under a pine tree. The hostel was surrounded by pines; the ground was covered with their long, sharp-looking needles, as if the trees were trying to lay down for us a loose, prickly carpet. Even where the bike path interrupted their encircling of the hostel, they'd managed to throw out a few branches, so that leaving or returning one had always to pass through the shaded, sharp-smelling tunnel they made.

As we mounted our bikes Amy came running from the hostel. "Wait," she called, and waved money and laughed. She was wearing her swimsuit. She'd pulled a T-shirt over it, but its orange bottom still peeked out from beneath its edge and looked alarmingly like underwear. We were sixteen, all of us, but none of us had had the courage to approach the girls on our trip. Instead we debated, whispering in our bunks at night, over whether any of them had approached any of us, and the only really sexual moments were the ones we shared ourselves, in the shower rooms, concealed comparisons which left us, depending on their outcomes, either jealous or sympathetic.

Amy was the prettiest of the girls. She had blond hair and a wide, bright face. Seeing she'd caught us, she stopped running, and took the last few steps at a walk. Her tan, I noticed, ended right below the joints of her hips, as if it were a pair of very high boots she'd just pulled on. "Where're you guys going?" she asked. She shaded her eyes before the sun, which, happily, had chosen that moment to make its reappearance.

"Supermarket," Eric said. "Why?"

She came closer. "Could you pick us up something?" she asked. "Could you? Just some Tab or some potato chips or something."

Eric nodded. "Sure," he said. He smiled, a surprise.

She looked at Jon and me. "You don't mind? Just some soda and stuff?" To Eric: "Just a bottle of Tab and some Ruffles or something."

Eric said, "Fine."

"Great," she said. She squinted, bringing her hand up again. With the other, she gave Eric a few folded dollar bills. "Just some Ruffles or Doritos or something. If they don't have either of those two then just pick up some cheese doodles." I made an exasperated noise, kicking at my pedal. Amy looked at me. "Is that okay? I mean, are you sure you can carry it with all the other stuff?"

"Oh, sure," Eric said, "we can carry it."

"Great. I mean, you know, we all really appreciate it. You know."

Jon and I turned to leave. "Hey," Eric said. Amy had turned to walk back to the hostel, and now she turned back around. "You want to come with us?" This surprised me. The evening I had been imagining, the three of us biking down the darkening highway, our spirits quiet and high, abruptly evaporated.

"What?" she asked, taking a few steps back.

Eric looked at Jon and me. "You want to come with us?"

She shook her head. "Can't. I got burned today. See?" She lifted one leg, showing Eric the inner part. It was lightly red. She traced her finger over the red part. "Here too, see?" She peeled the sleeve of her shirt back to reveal a cherry shoulder.

Eric had bent forward to look. "I hope it's okay," he said.

"Oh, it doesn't hurt or anything. It'll probably be gone by tomorrow."

"We'll just pick up your Doritos, then."

"Ruffles," she said. "If they have them, I guess." She walked back into the hostel.

We kicked up onto our pedals. Up the bike path, then. A thin concrete strip between the trees. It was littered with wood junk, twigs and pine needles, crushed acorn heads (the lost berets of dwarves) and sticky green pinecones. On either side, where the asphalt met the dirt, there were narrow gullies of fine light brown sand. Eric rode a little ahead of us. Jon and I pedaled behind, keeping a synchronized pace. Standing on our pedals we glided forward, our chains clicking and jangling as we flicked them from gear to gear. The day was beginning to die, and so we rode with exaggerated speed, as if to elude the moment when the sun and moon, in their nightly balancing act, would reverse places. The bike path was a roller coaster, low and then high, and we took the big hills giddily, took the sharp turns with an ease devised to satisfy only each other. The bike path ran parallel to the road, occasionally coming within just a few trees of it. Then we could hear the cars going by. This discouraged us, for with a roar the cars made a joke of the speed we took such pleasure in.

We were in town a little after six. There was a certain joy to seeing the town, to emerging from around the road's bend and seeing the clustered cars. It was a reminder that the world was still structured, that although we were on vacation there were still some people who drove and others who sold them gasoline. Many of the cars had their tops down, and most had radios. Separated by age and style, though, they were tuned to different stations, and so as we passed we heard two or three songs at once. Eric wove through the cars, getting farther and farther away from us.

We decided to go to the beach. Jon and I rode up to Eric to tell him. "We can't go," Eric said. "The supermarket closes at six-thirty." I told him we could probably pick up some hamburgers somewhere else, and Jon said flatly, "We're going." Eric still didn't want to go—in his eyes were the girls' snacks, and I remembered how, on the beach, he had stood at the edge of their circle, while Jon and I walked along the water and Matthew lay crackling on his towel alone—but we rode off ahead of him and, in passing the white-shingled A&P, the matter was more or less decided.

We came over the top of a low hill, and the sea appeared before us. We took the turn off Main Street without brakes and skimmed down a dark street where the sun could not be seen at all, blocked out by trees so old and tall they'd formed a canopy. The chill was on us, and we shivered: a smell of cool dirt, our arms producing tiny round goose bumps which made their hairs stand up. Eric, frowning, passed us and led us down roads which led to the beach. Jon and I spoke to him but he, sourly, did not answer. He stood a bit in his seat and lifted his rump to us as he pedaled more quickly. We followed and turned and the trees disappeared, ended abruptly with the corner, and then we were on a long wide road, flat, leading down towards the tops of the dunes. The sun was above us again with a slash of heat. On both sides of the road were patches of yellow silt, and beyond them high, green-and-yellow grass. Crickets hummed and clicked steadily. The traffic came in a slow stream towards us, trucks and station wagons and sports cars creeping back towards town in a long line. In a van two young men with beer cans hooted at us. From the payload of a pickup a group of girls waved. We waved back as the truck, encountering some dip in the road, lurched, and a few of them—their faces assuming expressions they might have worn were they to swallow something by mistake—clutched at the truck's sides. Eric's shirt had become untucked and the wind continually smoothed it out, sent quick wrinkles flaring down his back towards the tail, where they left for the air. The grass on our sides grew higher, thicker, until it was sea grass, reedy and sharp-looking. Its odor was acid-sour, choppy, and then a moment later its smell was replaced by the ocean's. Two dunes, sloping in towards the road, were the gate to the parking lot.

We did not lock our bikes but leaned them against a

splintering log where a few others had been chained. It felt strange to walk again, even stranger to walk across the sand which, with lazy effort, kept trying to swallow my feet. I pulled off my sneakers and dropped them next to my bicycle. Eric and Jon had walked on ahead of me, Eric a little ahead of Jon, and I ran to catch up, the sand kicking up from my heels as I went.

We hiked our shirts off over our heads, Jon and I, and ran for the water. The sand turned wet and hard beneath my feet—my last feeling was of it squeezing up between my first and big toes—and then with a shout I leapt into the water. Inside, I heard a similar explosion, and opening my eyes saw Jon flailing in the water beside me, his hair undulating around his head. We broke back to the surface and the clouds were over both our heads and I noticed, with a slight, sudden fear, that the sun had sunk a notch further. We swam along the shore for a while, just beyond the point where the waves could disturb us, where the gatherings of waves, the beginnings of waves, lifted us as we swam, pushed us a little higher in the water and then set us back down again. Treading water, we watched as Eric unbuttoned his oxford, a small figure on the shore. He took off his glasses, placed them on top of his spread shirt, and then trotted out into the water, pushed through one wave, then another, until he was bobbing beside us, smiling, spitting a little unwanted ocean from his mouth.

RELATIVITY

WHEN ROSS TIFTON ARRIVED AT Brown University for the first time, in late August, he found that there was somebody else already living in his room. The number on his key said 216, but when Ross opened the door to 216, there the other person's stuff was. The bookshelf was full, the bed was made. On the wall was a poster Ross had seen before: two teams of soccer players on top of a tall cliff in the middle of the ocean, two of them looking over the edge, perplexed, their black-and-white ball floating in the water hundreds of feet below. What Ross had always wondered about the poster was how the soccer players had gotten on top of the cliff in the first place. If they'd helicoptered up (the only real option), couldn't they just radio the pilot and get the same helicopter to fly over and rescue the ball?

"This isn't my room," Ross said, to his mother.

"That's certainly clear," Mrs. Tifton said. Helping Ross lug his bags had made her irritable. She just wanted to get someplace where she could put them down. She stuck her head into the room. After a moment she said, "You should make friends with this person. They're reading *Ulysses.*"

Joyce's book, Ross saw, was lying face down on the shelf, open to its exact middle like a fat butterfly.

"That doesn't mean anything," he said quickly. He wished his mother wouldn't say things like that. Ross believed that if people knew you needed friends, the odds were you weren't going to get any.

They left Ross's bags in the hall and walked down to Pembroke Residential Life. Ross explained his problem to the black woman behind the counter there. She was short with Ross, as though the doubling-up situation were somehow his fault—he was creating a problem where there was none, was the clear implication. When she looked his name up on her clipboard, however, she discovered that Ross's room was really 210. They exchanged keys. "Things are so hectic around now," she explained, apologizing, "you should feel lucky to have a room at all." In the middle of this, Ross's mother went off to a pay phone to call New York. Throughout the summer, Ross had toyed with the idea of not having her drive him to school at all. Mrs. Tifton ran a gallery on West 57th Street—she had a knack for turning any trip into a business venture. Everywhere they went, she turned out to know artists or collectors. Ross had a recurring nightmare in which he went to the hospital. His mother came to visit, but instead of sitting by his bedside she spent all her time going to other floors, visiting artists and collectors who happened to be in the hospital too.

After they'd unpacked, Ross walked his mother back to her car, which was parked on Brown Street, under a dogwood tree. Ross kissed her good-bye, then stood by the window while she started the engine.

"It's a beautiful campus," Mrs. Tifton said. "You'll be very happy here, I know." It felt to Ross, suddenly, as if she were selling him an artwork which, once bought, could only decline in value. He picked a dogwood petal off the hood of her car and tore it in half, the slight juice wetting his fingertips. They kissed again through the window, and then Mrs. Tifton drove off, her window rising with an electric smoothness.

Back in the dorm, Ross knocked on 216. He wanted to apologize for having gone into the guy's room without asking. His real reason, though, was that he wanted to meet whoever it was who lived there. Maybe his mother was right, and *Ulysses* was a good sign. No one answered, so Ross walked back to his own room, wrote out a short note, and taped it to 216's door. Then he went to dinner. Ross was a transfer to Brown. He'd transferred from Earlham College, a small school in Richmond, Indiana, and one of the main reasons he'd transferred was that he could see how much pain the place gave his mother. Ross knew that, on a certain level, people bought art to impress their dealers. The dealer presented herself as a woman of taste and style, someone whose judgments mattered, and her clients, by buying what she suggested, felt they were moving a step closer into her world. Everything about Mrs. Tifton made her perfect for this role. She lived in the East 80s, was married to an investment lawyer. When Ross was younger, she'd had a son at Dalton. The only slip had been his college. When Ross was at Dalton, Mrs. Tifton had mentioned him at openings all the time. Now, he had noticed, she hardly mentioned him at all. When her more established clients asked the name of her son's school, Mrs. Tifton would say, almost as a question, "Earlham?" The question was, Had they heard of it? None had. Their eyes would dart around, like surveyors adjusting to a surprising element in a familiar landscape, and Ross had the confusing idea, during his first year at Earlham, that he was affecting not so much his own career as his

RELATIVITY

mother's. He could tell that when Brown accepted him, she was elated. She took him to Brooks Brothers, and they spent the afternoon there, shopping, in celebration.

Ross had his own, private reasons for coming to Brown. Films and books he'd seen and read in high school had given him a clear picture of what college would be like. Reading *The Great Gatsby*, he'd been struck particularly by the train ride home from New Haven, the gallant, sophisticated students stalking through the train stations of the old Northeast. Ross wanted there to be train stations, tall trees, Georgian buildings, mammoth libraries with ceilings like inverted ship-hulls. Earlham's campus was composed mainly of a series of interlocking parking lots. Ross spent his time there studying, going up and speaking with his professors after class, ostensibly to clear up various tricky points in the lecture but really to show how motivated he was, so they would be able to write convincing recommendations for him later, when the time came.

At Dalton, surrounded by wealthy, handsome kids, Ross had felt he was floating on a kind of shiny dirigible into the future: these kids were going places. It was the opposite of the slaggy feeling he'd had at Earlham, where everyone seemed to be traveling in a beat-up Ford, something to park quietly and then slip away from as quickly as possible. Ross wanted to again meet students who carried their bright future successes around with them, in a magic halo that would enlarge to include anyone standing nearby. He'd come to Brown to make friends, and that was why his mother's remark had upset him. It was why he'd put the note on 216's door.

Later that evening, Ross was awakened by a pounding on his own door. It was after midnight. Ross said, "Just a minute," found his bathrobe, and opened the door. The person in his doorway was very tall, and stood very straight.

22

He had shaggy hair, a pushed-forward forehead, and a heavy jaw. Ross was aware of himself squinting in the bright light from the hallway.

"I'm Tom Creely," the person said. He pointed with his thumb down the hall, chuckled. "I live in 216. You left a note saying there was some problem with my room?"

Tom's voice was very deep, and Ross felt his own was scratchy and high in comparison. He knew instantly that he didn't want to be friends with this person. He seemed off, somehow—maybe in the way he stood. "I just wanted to apologize for walking in without asking, was all," Ross said.

"Are we supposed to be roommates or something?"

"No. This is my room. It was a mix-up, and I wanted to apologize."

"You're a senior?" Tom shifted his weight from one leg to the other.

"Junior. I'm a transfer."

"Really?" Tom said. "Me too." He nodded, as if this confirmed something. Then, as if finally noticing from Ross's face that he didn't want the conversation to continue, but unwilling to let him end it himself, Tom looked down the hall and said, "Well, shit. I have to go. It was nice meeting you, Ross. See you around." He chuckled, and they shook hands. This was how Ross met Tom Creely.

There were two other transfers on the hall. Peter Abrahms lived next door to Tom, a short, already balding boy from the University of Chicago. He had the diffidence very intelligent people have, but also an alertness. When he listened to you, he'd cock his head, and his eyes would travel all over your face, as if he were tracking your actual words through the air, noting their size and trajectory.

Mark Caron—tall, curly-haired, thin, born and raised in

Minnesota—came from Stanford. He'd left because things hadn't seemed quite right to him there. It was hard to remember you were in college under the flat California sunshine, difficult to study in the Spanish-style buildings, in which, he explained, you felt more like a monk or rancher than a student. What he was saying, of course, was that even though Stanford had a higher ranking, he'd come to Brown for many of the same reasons Ross had. Ross liked him immediately.

Ross liked both Mark and Peter. Mark was smart, if not quick—steady. He was uneasy about generalizing, which is the heart of cleverness. He had instead that cautious midwestern desire to know the facts. People from the East, Ross knew, didn't want to know too many facts. They skittered over their lives and decisions like water flies dancing over the scum of a pond, and an abundance of detail would sink them. People from the West—Peter was from Oregon— didn't need any facts at all. Between these two poles sagged the plodding Midwest. By the end of their first week, Ross had assigned them roles. Peter—with his tiny bald spot, as if his superior mental firepower were singeing the hair from his head—would be his intellectual friend. Mark—with his turtlenecks—would be his social one. Ross had inherited from his mother the idea that friends were, in a certain sense, props by which you were judged. He felt no compunction being judged on the basis of Mark and Peter. But he did feel uneasy being judged on the basis of Tom. Tom, in his work boots and T-shirts (most bearing the names of southern rock bands; like the slight accent in his voice, they were an accessory he'd picked up at the University of Jacksonville), was an embarrassment. At parties, he would dance so violently everyone would turn to look. In the library, he would talk and talk. But there was no way to hang around Mark and Peter without also hanging around Tom. Both were adamant about this—Peter, because he and Tom were already friends (they'd arrived at Brown early), and Mark because he felt that the four transfers on Miller Hall should stick together.

To his surprise, Ross discovered that his dislike was reciprocal. As September progressed, Tom became increasingly vocal about his feelings for Ross. Tom seemed to have bought wholeheartedly the image of himself Ross was trying to project. And since people like Ross had always rejected Tom, Tom had decided, as much as was possible within the confines of their "friendship," that he would reject Ross. When Ross brushed his hair in the bathroom, Tom would say, "Jesus, Tifton loves himself." At dinner in the Vernon-Woolley, Mark and Peter both being Political Science concentrators (Ross and Tom were in English), they would talk about current events. Tom would keep silent. Peter would lead off with something provocatively liberal, like not only should we stop supporting the contras in Nicaragua, we should actually begin funding the Sandinistas. He had confessed to them, with a smile, that he felt it was his duty to produce challenging ideas. Mark—who, being from the Midwest, was perhaps geographically inclined to conservatism—would say, "We don't need a Soviet beachhead in Central America." Ross would counter with something centrist, and only then would Tom jump in. He'd disagree with Ross so stridently and so loudly that pretty girls from other tables would glance over at them, to see what the commotion was.

By the third week of September, Ross had decided that he wasn't going to hang around Tom anymore. But he couldn't find a way out. When he suggested to Mark and Peter, on those evenings when Tom was late coming back from class, that they go to dinner without their tall, noisy friend, he'd receive only hurt, uncomprehending stares, as if he'd just suggested they go butcher a harp seal. "He really likes you, Ross," Peter would say. Mark would say, "Come on, Ross. We don't want to have bad feelings on the hall." Ross didn't care. Tom was loud, abusive, unfriendly. "Plus, he smells." They'd all commented on the fact that, as a component of his own grungy style, Tom seemed to shower only two or three times a week. Peter and Mark would blink. Ross guessed that some of what he said might get back to Tom, but he didn't care. What was the worst that could happen? Tom wouldn't want to be friends with him anymore?

That Friday, there was a special section in the *Brown Daily Herald* on fashions at Brown. It was a silly article, discussing the variety of different clothing worn by the students. *Herald* photographers had searched the campus for "those students best exemplifying current fashion trends at Brown." There were three pictures. First was a boy in patched jeans and a bandanna, in blurry action, catching a Frisbee on the Green. "Activist," said the caption. Next was a girl in a black sweater and black dress, with dyed hair and dark, tortuous-looking boots. Her lit cigarette had also been colored-in black, but clumsily, so readers could see it had been done. "Semiotician," said the caption. "Note footwear." The semi-oticians, Ross had gathered, did something dark and complex with film, searching for the same sorts of hidden, symbolic structures kids in high school had claimed to find in television commercials. The biggest photo, in the middle of the page, said, "Classic." It was Ross. He was wearing his argyle vest, a blue blazer, and a scarf. Ross was tremendously excited; it was like an official welcome to Brown. He went back to the stand where the *Herald*s were distributed and took ten extra copies, to mail to his parents and to different friends.

Back in the dorm, Mark and Peter teased him about the photo all afternoon. At dinner, Tom kept calling him "Mr. Classic." Whenever anyone walked by their table, Tom would say, in a loud voice, "Boy, I bet the person going past us now doesn't realize he's right next to Mr. Classic." Ross asked Tom to cut it out. "What's the matter?" Tom asked. "Afraid for people to know what a famous guy you are? Afraid that girl right over there will find out that you're Mr. Classic?" Ross stopped talking. He finished dinner early and left the table, saying good-bye to everyone but Tom. Back in his room, he started *The Sound and the Fury*, which he had to read for comparative literature class (Proust, Joyce, and Faulkner). At seven, when everyone came back from the V-W, Ross heard Tom outside his door: "Shh. Everyone be quiet. We don't want to disturb Mr. Classic. He's probably in there feeding his shirts or something." Around eleven, as Ross was getting ready for bed, he heard Tom singing in the hall. Ross ignored it, until he realized the song was about him.

"He's a collegiate kind of guy," Tom sang. "He looks pretty good, in his loafers and stuff, and he always gets going when the going gets tough, he's a collegiate kind of guy. Ross Tifton's a collegiate kind of guy. Mr. Classic by day, so people will say, he's a collegiate kind of guy."

Ross was sure everyone on the hall could hear. He threw open his door. Tom was halfway down the hall, taping a copy of the *Herald* to the wall. He'd drawn a thin half-oval at the groin of Ross's photo, with a circle on either side and a line on the tip. With a thick, felt-tip pen, he'd changed the caption from "Classic" to "Mr. Classic's Penis." There was a large, scratchy arrow pointing to the rather modest set of genitalia he'd given Ross. Ross wasn't sure how to respond. He could have laughed the whole thing off, or said "Cut it out," again. Months later, he would actually sit down and calculate the large number of options he'd had. But when Tom saw Ross, he widened his eyes in mock fear and hunched into a fighter's stance. Ross had the idea that perhaps what Tom wanted was some kind of physical contact. Maybe if Ross proved he was a man, or whatever, Tom would gain respect for him and leave him alone. Maybe it was another part of his southern code. So Ross rushed him. Tom grabbed his arms, lifted him up, and the next thing Ross knew he was lying flat across Tom's shoulders. Tom was spinning him around, banging his arms and feet against the plaster of the wall. Ross was afraid. But then the next moment Tom threw him to the floor, and Ross, flying, realized he was okay, that Tom was throwing him out of his life, that he was giving Ross an excuse never to have to talk to him again.

Ross didn't tell his parents what had happened, when they called on Sunday. But he didn't send them the *Herald* article, either. The experience with Tom had dirtied it, somehow—Ross couldn't see the word "Classic" without also seeing "Mr." and "Penis" around it. It was too bad, because the clipping was just the sort of thing his mother liked. She would have hung it on the wall of her office, to show to clients in case any of them made it that far back.

He did tell Mark and Peter, though. He felt good, over lunch, relating the details. In fact, he had to physically restrain himself from smiling. Tom had given him a good, solid out. "You know what I realized? When I was up there spinning around?" he asked. Neither boy answered. "Tom's crazy. You saw that drawing he put on the wall. He's nuts."

"I wouldn't say he was crazy, exactly," Mark said, cautiously.

"What I don't understand," Peter said, with a quick hand gesture as if waving away the issue, a conversational parking attendant motioning the next topic forward, "is what you're so happy about, Ross."

"I'm not happy," Ross said.

But he was happy, and there was nothing he could really do to contain himself. He stopped hanging around Tom completely. It was October. Students around campus were wearing their fall clothes. Everyone looked good, put together, in the way Ross had imagined. There was a crispness to the air which reminded Ross of the smell of apples, the sharp scent they spray up with the first chunky bite. The grayness of cloudy days, the slight saltiness in the mist (Providence sat just upstream from the Narragansett Bay), all contributed to Ross's happiness. Walking the campus, Ross felt as if he were a hawk, floating over the life he'd wanted to lead. The correct folding of his wings, a sudden drop in wind pressure, and he'd land in the world he'd wished to inhabit. He imagined what would have happened if he hadn't fought with Tom—a year of gray, embarrassing dinners at the V-W. He couldn't help feeling he'd made a narrow escape. On the pages of books from the Rockefeller Library were tiny flecks of red ink. When you closed these books completely, the specks would merge to spell out the words *Brown University Library*. This was how Ross saw his days. Each held a little fleck of feeling which, when pressed together by his memory at some later date, would combine to tell him exactly how he'd felt. He ate lunch with Mark and Peter, who tried to convince him to give Tom a second chance. "He feels bad about what happened," Peter said. Ross shook his head. He'd become friendly with another boy on the hall, John Erhenkrantz. John had dark hair and an almost embarrassingly perfect nose, absolutely straight like the nose of a hero in a children's cartoon. After Ross had known him a few weeks, John confessed that this nose was not his own. He'd had a job right after high school, as a graduation present. Mark got along with John, too, and the three of them would go out to eat together, at restaurants on Thayer Street.

The weekend before Thanksgiving, John organized a touch-football game. Ross knew he shouldn't play the minute he heard Tom was—Mark had invited him, to keep the hall together—but he wanted to. Anyway, the game might be an opportunity for him and Tom to make up, for Ross to show that, now that their connection was severed, he had no hard feelings. Ross put on sweatpants, a rugby shirt, and tramped over to Pembroke field. When Tom saw him, he said, "Look, Tifton's trying to get his picture in the application booklet." Ross laughed with everyone else. What he'd forgotten was how big Tom actually was. In his mind, Tom had become reduced to an irritating, faintly comic obstacle. Looking at him now, in his jeans and T-shirt, Ross remembered that Tom was a physical being, and a large one at that.

They ended up on separate teams, and the minute the game began, Ross knew he was in trouble. As Ross ran by him, Tom yelled, "I've got you, Tifton. You're mine." When he caught the ball, instead of tagging him, Tom tackled him to the ground. John helped Ross up, explained to Tom that the game was two-hand touch, not tackle. Tom nodded, but a down later, when Ross caught another pass, Tom yelled, "Look out, Mr. Classic," and tackled him again. Everyone—especially Mark—began to look uneasy. It wasn't clear if Tom was being serious. Ross was angry. On offense, when Tom had the ball, he would lower his head and run straight at Ross, a Creely torpedo. The next time Ross had the ball, he made it to midfield before John tagged him. The play was clearly over—Ross had already tossed the ball to John—when Tom said, "Tifton." Ross looked up and Tom tackled him, knocking him down into the wet leaves and mud. Ross threw Tom off, stood up, and then Tom tackled him again, and again. Tom wouldn't stop tackling him. John and a few other players grabbed Tom, holding him away.

"I'm leaving, okay?" Mark said. He was standing at the other end of the field, picking up his sweatshirt. Ross said, "Me too." He looked at Peter, who shrugged, meaning he was staying. As Ross and Mark walked away, Tom called, "What's the matter with you two babies, huh? Afraid of a little football? Afraid to play, Ross?" Mark didn't speak for the rest of the afternoon. He seemed much more upset, to Ross, than Ross was himself. Ross felt fine. He was right; Creely really was crazy. He wasn't worried about him. There were people in his building in New York he hadn't spoken to for years, so there seemed no reason he couldn't keep away from Tom. At dinner, Mark seemed to be considering something. Finally, he said he was sorry. Ross knew very well what he was apologizing for, but he said, with an it's-okay shrug, "No, it's fine. You don't have to talk, if you don't want to." Mark said, with a little smile, "You know what I mean." Ross said, "No," but he felt his own smile was giving him away. Mark laughed, and then Ross laughed too, both with their heads lowered, as if they were sharing a guilty secret. Mark stopped talking to Tom in the days before Thanksgiving.

Thanksgiving dragged finals in after it, like a last course. School took up most of their time. At progressive Brown, there were fewer exams than papers. In each class, Ross's professors benignly announced, "We want to measure what you *do* know, not what you don't." Mark missed exams;

they were, he felt, the only drama you had as a student. Ross agreed. Papers were just time-consuming and hallucinatory. He had a twenty-pager due in Proust, Joyce, and Faulkner. Time became a thing measured not in hours but in pages. After a certain point, his words stopped making sense, even to Ross. He felt as if he were being blanketed in his words, wrapped up and tossed struggling into pools of paragraphs, where white pages darted by like skittish fish. It was difficult to imagine the actual, Christmastime world of New York— the huge snowball suspended over 57th and Fifth, the great origami Christmas tree at the Museum of Natural History— through the haze of sentences he would have to write, reread, and correct. Friday night, for a break, John suggested they go see *It's a Wonderful Life,* which the Brown Film Society always showed around Christmas. Peter couldn't go, and this time not even Mark suggested inviting Tom. They went, and it was vivifying, for Ross, to see the good people acting correctly and having nice things happen to them. He liked how Jimmy Stewart was supposed to be a good man but was still allowed to get angry at the bad characters in the film and give them their due. After the film, John—actually sniffling—hugged Ross and Mark. "This always happens to me," he explained. John would be studying in London the following term, so the evening was a kind of good-bye. They went out for coffee, then walked back through the night— the streetlights had little halos, from the cold—with their hands in their pockets. Ross was happy. If Tom had been with them, the evening would have been an embarrassment (how would Tom have reacted, for example, to being hugged by John Erhenkrantz?). As it was, Ross felt the wind pressure in his life was changing.

Around midnight, Peter ran out of paper and began asking if anyone else had any. Ross had just opened a fresh turquoise box of Eaton's Berkshire Bond. He called, "In here, Peter." The next thing he heard was Tom's voice, followed by a kind of scuffle. Mark yelled, "Hey, Tom! Cut it out!" Then there was a lot of thumping. Ross ran to his door. Mark was twisted up on the floor of the hall, with Tom crouched over him, grimacing, pressing down. Tom had his hands on Mark's head and was banging it against the ground. John had come out of his room also. When Tom saw them, he let go, jumped up, shouted down at Mark, "You were trying to kill me," and ran down the hall to his room, shutting and, with an oily clunk, locking the door behind him.

Ross and John helped Mark up. In his room, Mark sat at his desk without talking. He would occasionally shake his head, as if mentally testing out various propositions, and rejecting them. Finally, he looked up and said, "We have to get Creely out of here." His eyes were rimmed with red. He'd been, without Ross's noticing it, crying.

What had happened was that Peter had asked for paper. Mark had come out into the hall. Then Ross said he had some. Mark had turned around, and Tom said, "Go ahead. Why don't you answer your lover?" Here Mark imitated Tom's voice, the super-straight way he held his head while speaking, the expulsion of each word rocking his head back with the counterforce of release. Then Tom pushed Mark in the back. Mark felt he had to do something, so he turned around and pushed back. Tom said, "Oh, you want to go at it, Caron?" and the next thing Mark knew, he was on the ground and Tom was banging his head against the floor. "You can't live with a person like that," Mark said. "He's crazy. Ross tried living with him, and look what happened at the football game. We've got to get him out of here."

Ross didn't like the idea. If Tom really was unglued, who

knew how he'd react if they had him kicked out? Ross didn't want to go through life afraid of Tom Creely. "I don't care," Mark said, shaking his head. "I just want him out of here." Mark was crying again, and Ross felt a depressing sense of responsibility. If Ross hadn't been on the hall, he felt, Mark would never have gotten beat up.

Ross and John finally convinced Mark to call his parents before doing anything, and, in the end, it was his parents who convinced him not to. Around one-thirty Mark knocked on Ross's door and came into his room. His words had the clear, decisive sound of a parent at the generating end. There were only a few days left in the term. He'd avoid Tom, and if things started up again in the spring, well, he could decide then. He didn't have time to waste now. Mark thanked Ross for helping him, said good night, and went back to his room. Ross realized, shifting in bed, doing a little internal monitoring, that his bleak feeling had broken up; he was happy again. It had been at the back of his mind all semester that Tom had been, somehow, specifically attracted to him. When Ross was a boy, walking the streets of Manhattan with his mother, Mrs. Tifton had accused him of attracting vagrants and bag ladies. Ross protested he didn't, and his mother would say, "You *do*, by looking at them." Ross had worried that it was this propensity of his that had brought Tom upon him. Now he saw this was out of the question. He was blameless, Tom was crazy. Ross felt as if a heaviness had been lifted from him. They would return from vacation, pick out new courses, and never have anything to do with Tom again. He had succeeded in having Tom Creely completely removed from his life.

The Tiftons never went away for Christmas. The holidays were an important time for Mrs. Tifton's gallery. Collectors flew in from Europe and California, and Mrs. Tifton had to be on hand to greet them. Mr. Tifton was at his office all day, so Ross had the long Brown vacation—over a month—to spend on his own.

He spent it at parties—parties of high school friends, of people from Earlham, of people he'd met at Brown. Ross was an arriviste at Brown, with an arriviste's secret fear that the place he'd arrived at actually was worthless—it had, after all, stooped to admit him—and also the converse fear that people were jealous of his good fortune, and that he had to take it easy on them. At parties with Earlham friends, Ross would explain that there was little difference between the two schools: teachers, facilities, students, all were the same. At parties with other friends, he'd admit, after suitable prompting, that there was nothing like the Ivy League, that nowhere else was a college. With clients at his mom's gallery, he'd simply say the name "Brown" and they'd simply nod, like professors in class when you've given the right—if not necessarily surprising—answer.

At parties with Dalton friends, Ross met other people from Brown. He was excited; he was widening his social circle. These new people, he discovered, lived not in the "good" dorms on campus but off campus entirely, in rented houses and apartments all over College Hill. "You live on campus?" they'd ask coolly, in the same tone of voice people at his mother's gallery asked if you owned an Andrew Wyeth or a Ben Shahn. Ross took phone numbers and addresses.

A week before classes resumed, Ross's mother sat him down in her office and asked how things were going. Something in the aggressive tilt of her crossed legs made it clear—this was to be their confidential talk. Ross could even picture it in her appointment calendar—"2:30: Talk w/ Ross." He told her as much as he felt comfortable about the school, his friends. He didn't mention the situation with Tom at all. He didn't want it marring her vision—otherwise, she'd think of Brown, and what she'd see would be Tom Creely. Plus, what use could she have for the information? "Oh, your son had trouble with a lunatic at Dartmouth? My son had trouble with a lunatic at Brown." Ross's grades arrived. He had three A's and a B. His mother hugged him, said, "I'm so proud of you," and took him back to Brooks Brothers again for more clothing. His father shook his hand with a little grimace of appreciation and said, "I knew you could handle anything, Ross," which instead implied the opposite, that there had in fact been some anxiety about his ability to perform at Brown. By the middle of January, Ross was ready to return to Providence.

And, for the first few days, it was nice being back. Ross felt a connection to the school. The trees, leafless, looked stark and lovely on the green. A bright spotlight of sun falling on, say, a patch of ice at the corner of University Hall would reassure Ross that he was in the right place. Tom was ignoring them. If one of them was brushing his teeth when Tom, in his dusky red towel, came to use the shower, he'd wheel around on his heel and thump on up to the upstairs bathroom without a word. They ate lunch with Peter, who told them things were okay, Tom had no hard feelings towards either of them. "He still likes both of you guys," Peter said. At dinner, Peter ate with Tom and Mark ate with Ross. So at mealtimes, at least, the hall was now officially divided.

But to Ross's dismay, he discovered that Tom was in two of his classes. Both were courses Ross needed for his concentration (Nineteenth-Century British Fiction, Brontë to Conrad; American Literature II, The Modern Imagination), so there was no question of his dropping them. The first day, Tom walked in and took a seat in the region behind Ross. For eighty minutes, Ross could feel the anger circling around his neck, exploring the contours of his head, as if Tom's rage were making a casting of his skull. The hall felt odder. There was a new student in John Erhenkrantz's room, a tall, quiet Egyptian boy with a range of acne on one cheek. This Egyptian and a Filipino student had decided they didn't like the V-W, and had taken to cooking meals in their own rooms, using the Egyptian boy's microwave or else a hot plate. Ross would walk into the bathroom and find them dumping boiling spaghetti water into the sink (the mirror fogging in a widening circle), or else gutting a fish, pushing the glucky remains down into the drain with their fingers. One morning, Ross looked down to see two slivers of mushroom and the back end of a carrot floating in the soapy water into which he'd just dipped his razor.

The afternoon of the Super Bowl, Tom walked into Mark's room. Ross and Mark were watching the pre-game. Neither had spoken a word to Tom all term, and it was intimidating to have his large presence suddenly before them. "You guys mind if I watch the big game?" he asked. He looked at them with a quick, half-defensive smile. It was a clear message—he was willing to call off hostilities if they were.

And it seemed to Ross as if the whole year were on the line. To become friendly with Tom again would be to restart the whole depressing cycle; all the progress they'd made last term would be lost, they'd be stuck with Tom Creely again. Ross looked at Mark, who seemed frozen between his anger at what had happened and his good American impulse to dole out a second chance. Ross imagined the Midwest was a place where second chances grew pretty freely, on corn-stalks. He caught Mark's eye and shook his head, trying to put into his expression the words *Remember, this is the guy who banged your head against the floor.*

So, after a moment, Mark said, "Well, actually, Tom, we kind of do."

Tom's eyes narrowed. "Why?" he asked, lowly.

"Well, look," Mark said, his tone shifting, feeling more comfortable with facts to stand behind and lean on, "a lot of bad things happened last term. We all got into fights. You had fights with Ross, you and I had that thing in the hall, remember? I'm not saying it's anyone's fault."

"Well, I'm willing to forget it," Tom said. "Can't you guys forget it?" He clenched and unclenched his jaw. The muscle showed through the skin of his face like a guppy's beating heart.

"But it didn't happen to you," Ross said. He didn't think it fair for Mark to do all the talking, and anyway this was an important distinction. "It happened to us.'"

Tom laughed, shaking his head, as if by moving he were slicing through numerous strands of irritating detail. "Are you asking me to leave your room, Mark?" he asked. He looked at Mark coldly.

Mark's voice sped up. "Look, all I'm saying is that maybe we should all try to think about ways of avoiding our problems."

"Are you asking me to leave your room?" Tom asked.

There was a pause. Mark lowered his explaining hands. "Yes, Tom. I'm asking you to leave my room." Tom got up, looked at them, and left.

On Monday, the space shuttle exploded. All over campus, everyone spent the afternoon in their rooms, watching the news. The anchormen were playing with models, speculating. Satellite hookups allowed scientists in Washington to agree with engineers in Houston on the slim chances of anyone's surviving the blast. And they kept showing the same clip, the shuttle arching upward and then rolling over, like a basking whale. Ross wondered how the family of the teacher felt. It was the most obvious nightmare, the kind of thing, Ross thought, that they must have joked about beforehand. The one flight she goes on is the one to explode in mid-air. Ross watched sitting on the floor in Mark's room. Four times, Tom stomped by. Ross could feel the floorboards shaking under his hands. The slam of Tom's door was a wooden explosion.

The next morning, Ross had Brontë to Conrad. This time, he and Tom sat in the same row, Tom at one end and Ross at the other. Tom sat perfectly straight, his head floating above the others like a mountaintop poking through clouds. It was unbearable. No matter where Ross looked, there was Tom, stuck in the corner of his eye. He couldn't take notes. Something hot was revolving in his stomach. He wondered how anyone in class could fail to feel it, the hatred congealing in the air over their heads. Wednesday, when Ross came back from class, Mark was sitting at his desk with his door open. He looked upset. Ross had a sudden fear that Mark had tried to talk to Tom, and Tom, once again, had beaten him up. "What's the matter?" Ross asked.

Mark looked up. He had a paper in his hand. "The day after the shuttle," he said, "I wrote Tom a letter. I just said the same things we'd talked about, how the three of us couldn't get along, how it was nobody's fault. I put it under his door. Then, today, I found this under my door." He handed Ross the paper.

Mark:
You wrote me a letter. People return other people's letters. You gave me your thoughts. Now I'll give you mine.
In this game, there will always be challenges. Some

meet them head on. In my humble opinion, I feel that those who do are most worthy to live a full life. This may sound like utter insanity, which in fact it is. When we fought, I gained respect for you. The reason we fought, in my mind, was not so I could intimidate you. I saw a challenge in it, for myself as well as for you. It gave me the opportunity to see what you really feel inside, whether there was any fire or not. Perhaps I am an angry old bastard, but I never fight without a higher reason than just to see who is stronger or who's best or whatever.

This respect I have for you is because I had the opportunity to see what you were made of. This is a respect I can never have for Tifton, because when I was there looking the bull in the eyes I saw nothing. There was no fire, there was nothing, zip, null, negative. This disgusts me. I can't stand a person like that, and, if anything, I try to instill some fire in them because I think it is something that people need in order to truly experience life. I can't stand seeing someone floundering himself away with no feeling or passion. What then?

Now, what does all this mean? Well in my mind, I could never like Tifton because of what he is. You, however, I respect. A true remorse for sins committed against Mr. Tifton I have trouble with, for I cannot really convince myself I was genuinely wrong about that. If I had to live it over again? It would probably have gone just the same way. Wherever you may go Mark Caron, go with your heart first, feel with your heart, realize with your heart. Never give in to mediocrity.

Sincerely yours,
Thomas R. Creely

The next morning, of course, they went to see the dean first thing. They walked under Faunce Arch and across the stunted winter campus at eight-thirty. On the Green, a few students were standing in a circle with raised fists and white armbands, silently protesting the university's ties to South Africa. They weren't wearing jackets (Ross could see the lips of one girl twitching), and their willingness to suppress shivers seemed evidence of dedication. Ross wondered whether there was some way he and Mark could protest Tom. Frederic Sackler, dean of undergraduate counseling, was a small, thin man, with square-metal glasses and a mustache the mottled yellow-and-white of used cigarette filters. He shook their hands, then sat down behind his desk, using his palm to steady his tie. "Well," he said, "what can I do for you folks this fine February morning?"

It was Ross who spoke. The key was to appear as disinterested as possible; any hint of vengefulness, and the dean would suspect their motives for coming. It was like when his mother sold a painting; it if was too clear she wanted to sell, the buyer became uneasy. Ross spoke levelly. As the story came out, Dean Sackler looked from Ross to Mark, from Mark to Ross, with a merry expression, as if to say, "Well, yes, you've come to the right place, but what took you so long getting here?" Finally, Ross said, "We just haven't got time for this anymore. We just want to do our schoolwork." This line, he knew, irresistible to any dean, would be the coup de grâce.

When he handed the dean Tom's note, though, Ross felt a little twinge. It didn't seem fair to be showing it to the dean, someone it hadn't been addressed to. For a moment, Ross saw himself as on the wrong side, the evil character in a movie, turning someone in. He and Mark watched Dean Sackler read. After the first paragraph, the dean lifted his head with a surprised expression and said, "Well, we do have a situation here, don't we?" Then he dipped back into the letter. When he'd finished, he put the letter on his desk and leaned back in his chair, looking up at the ceiling with a deep, contemplative expression, as if in silent consultation with the light fixture. Finally, he snapped forward and said, "Look, fellows, there are several levels we can work on here." With his hands, he illustrated the concept of several levels. "One, we can have Tom brought immediately before the Board of Disciplinary Review. You can testify that he attacked you, we could have him out of here by the middle of next week. But I get the impression you two don't want that." He looked at them. When they shook their heads, he said, "Okay, Two: you guys go away for the weekend, we bring Tom in here, on Friday, for psychological testing. If our psychiatrist decided he was too unstable to stay, our hands would be tied. If not, I could still bring him into my office and give him a good scare. I can be a bulldog when I want to be. Now, do either of you have relatives in the area you could stay with, on the spur of the moment?"

Mark had a cousin at Wellesley. The dean laid out the plan. They'd leave Friday, before two-thirty. Dean Sackler would call Tom into his office at three. On Sunday, Ross would call the dean from Wellesley to find out what had happened. Shaking the dean's hand again, Ross could see that he was excited by their case. It was probably better than what he usually got, homesick foreign students or sullen, reformed athletes looking to get off academic probation. Outside in the cold morning, Ross and Mark didn't speak for a moment. They'd delivered the problem into official hands, but they felt the cold, queasy feeling conspirators must feel, after a plot has been settled on and all subtleties and second thoughts have been driven down, to clot the stomach.

What was strange was how, in retrospect, the weekend at Wellesley would stay in Ross's mind as one of the high points of the year. Mark's cousin had Mark's same curly hair, the same fleshiness to her upper lip. She was tall. Wellesley itself was lovely. The girls were pretty and seemed, somehow, younger than students in Providence. There was a pleasant feeling of dislocation Ross felt, walking with Mark, as if the two of them were floating in air above circumstances, the dean and Tom talking, Tom's insane letter. This dislocation seemed to translate itself into the campus. Saturday night it snowed, and the tall pine trees, with their shaggy, upraised arms, took on the look of molting birds. Mark and Ross and Mark's cousin went tray sledding down the hill behind the Wellesley library, and Ross seemed, his worry and his happiness merging, to be in a dream, or in one of those transitional states between dreams, where the details of one merge slowly into the details of another, producing an unnameable mood. Sunday morning, Ross woke at seven. Everyone else was sleeping, their clothes, still wet, fighting for space on the warm radiator. Ross was afraid, terrified, at the idea of returning to Brown. He repeated the words of Tom's letter to himself and realized that Tom was dangerous, a dangerous person. But then Mark's cousin turned over in her bed, and her new position started her snoring, and Ross felt safe, like Achilles run to hide on the island of women.

In the afternoon he called Dean Sackler. Mark sat by him, whispering, "Ask if he told Tom he'd done the wrong thing." It didn't seem wise to tell the dean how to do his job, so Ross just listened. Dean Sackler had called Tom into Rhode Island Hall on Friday. He'd been tested by one of the university psychiatrists. The tests had shown Tom to be non-psychotic, and the dean had spoken to him in his office. "He's still there," Ross whispered to Mark, covering the mouthpiece. Mark frowned. They'd both been hoping, se-

95

cretly, that the psychiatrist would take the initiative and kick Tom out. "I'd keep in touch with this fellow Peter," Dean Sackler said. "That way, if Creely starts boiling over again, you'll have a warning and you can call me and I can bring him back into my office." Ross asked, "Did you say to Tom his behavior was wrong?" and Mark nodded vigorously. The dean cleared his throat. "I told him it was wrong if he wanted to stay at this university," he said. There was a pause. "I think I scared him pretty well. There shouldn't be another incident." This "shouldn't" was the most troubling thing in the conversation; Ross didn't relay it to Mark. They drove back to Providence silently, their moods transitional again. The snow on the highway was wet and ragged, and drifted back and forth over the divider like a mirage. Back at Brown, it had already been swept from the walkways and pushed together into a number of large, greasy piles which, Ross knew, would remain intact till spring. In the darkness, they gleamed like primitive religious monuments. The hall was gloomily quiet. Peter told them later that Tom, knowing they were returning, had spent the afternoon singing "When the Saints Come Marching In."

They avoided the dorm as much as possible. There was no avoiding Tom in class, however, not for Ross. Tom was tall and vocal. Plus, to Ross's horror, the books in their courses began to mimic their problem. In Brontë to Conrad, the first book was *Wuthering Heights*. Reading it on his bed, Ross felt his stomach sink, imagining Tom reading the exact same pages in his own room three doors down. How could Tom not see himself as Heathcliff? How could he help but feel vindicated when, in the book, the author so clearly approved Heathcliff's persecution of the wimpy, rejecting Lintons? Nor was this only, as Ross had hoped, his own paranoia. Far from downplaying them, the class lectures centered on just these particular points. Heathcliff was justified in destroying Edgar Linton; Edgar represented the stifling conventionality of the middle class, a stifling which had killed the first Cathy and which threatened to kill all the Earnshaws by muffling—as with a blanket—their natural vitality. Tom, listening, revolved his jaw, as if actually ingesting this information. He raised his hand and asked, "So, what you're saying is that Brontë condones Heathcliff's wanting his revenge?" With his put-on accent, he sounded like Stonewall Jackson talking it over with General Lee, and Ross wondered how the professor could fail to hear the anger in Tom's voice. But the professor just touched her chin for a moment, then nodded, saying, "Yes, yes, I would have to say that's a valid reading." Ross's stomach sank further. In American Literature II, the first books were *Daisy Miller* and *Huckleberry Finn*. The lectures moved along similar lines. It was as though both professors had read Tom's letter; Huck couldn't bear normal behavior and was heroic for striking out on his own. Daisy, like Heathcliff, was effectively murdered by a middle class which couldn't find a place for her liveliness, her fire. Ross sank into his desk, imagining Tom rising up, bashing Ross's head in with his chair, the rest of the class placidly watching and the professor nodding, saying, "Yes, very good, 'A' work, splendid." The police would arrive, Tom would be let off, the judge accepting literary convictions as legitimate grounds for murder.

Nor did this torture end in the classes Ross shared with Tom. All over campus, social and political concerns were crowding into Ross's life. He went to the post office looking for mail, and found instead scores of multicolored posters stapled to the walls, announcing lectures on "Racism, Our American Heritage," or "A Helping Economy: Feminist

97

Ethnic Spirituality Among the Mesquite Indians." Where had Ross been last term? How had he missed it? He'd been so caught up in making friends, in establishing himself at Brown, that he simply hadn't paid attention to the rest of the campus. But now, as he avoided the hall he'd first cultivated, Ross found the same issues being played out everywhere. No one on campus could get along with anyone else. On the "Letters" page of the *Herald*, the Association of Fraternity Presidents wrote baiting letters to the Sarah Doyle Center, which were responded to by the Women's Political Task Force with vague, threatening petitions. The Latino Student Association attacked the Asian-American Student Alliance for misrepresenting their problems in its *Report on Minority Enrollment*. The dean of student affairs urged the community to "discover the racism within us," as if such a discovery were a plus, worth discovering, like hidden creativity. People wrote in discussing what they'd overheard other people say. At least one letter a week began:

> To the Two Young Men on Line at the Dining Hall:
> Perhaps you think it is funny—the joke you were telling on February 23rd—but let me assure you, to those who have been raped, or have friends who've been raped, aggravated sexual assault is no laughing matter.

Ross had always thought that, if you eavesdropped, you yourself were responsible for hearing something you didn't like. But in fact these letters were usually followed, a day or two later, by others backing them up:

> To the Author of the "Letter to the Two Young Men":
> Thank you for your letter. I'm sick and tired of listening to other people's insensitivity. When are certain people

at this university going to learn that certain things just aren't funny?

The black students on campus had formed two umbrella organizations, the Third World Coalition and the Organization of United African Peoples (a boy Ross had known at Dalton was president of the OUAP—he'd grown up near Ross, on East 87th Street). They were mostly concerned with the "Eurocentrism" of Brown's curriculum. The university, they felt, simply had no interest in the achievements of anyone other than white European males. "When are the institutional racists of this University going to start paying attention to the cultural contributions of the so-called 'Primitive Societies'? " they asked, showing a Picasso next to an African mask, to prove their point. Ross, thinking that some paintings might cheer him up, visited the List Art Center to see a show of early abstract art. Instead, in the lobby, he saw a show of student work entitled "Beauty Is in the Eye of the Eurocentric Beholder." The paintings were all of beautiful, powerful-looking black women being squashed out of picture frames by pretty blond white girls in frilly clothes. In one, *Say What?*, a poor black girl in tribal dress stared sufferingly out at the viewer from one end of a long canvas, while at the other a diamond-earringed white girl, oblivious, sang along with the music coming out of her Walkman.

Nor did anyone on campus find any of this odd. The administrators encouraged these displays, and enthusiastically invited outside experts to come in and judge for themselves Brown's commitment to "non–First World education." These reports were invariably negative, but Brown persisted in having them done anyway. Deans would write in to the *Herald*, "We appreciate the suggestions of the

Coalition on Academic Fairness, and look forward to imple-
menting them at the first reasonable opportunity."

In Ross's Shakespeare class, one student asked why so
many of the female characters had been "marginalized" and
"silenced" by the text. What she meant, it turned out, was
Why hadn't they been given more lines? Far from finding
this ridiculous, the professor invited discussion on the issue,
and so for the remainder of the period everyone spoke as if
the characters were real people, as if Shakespeare's oeuvre
were a giant classroom in which the playwright had
chosen—on the cruel bases of race and sex—to call on some
people but not on others. In American Literature II, a black
girl asked the professor why, in *Huck Finn*, the author had
deliberately left out half the human race. The professor
paused, then began to explain, delicately, that the runaway
Jim was in fact a model portrayal of a black man, the most
realistic of its period. The girl shook her head firmly and
said, "No, I mean women." The professor was at a loss. He
finally invited discussion, and Ross felt it was stupid to point
out that the story Twain had chosen to tell was about two
men on a raft. Literature, after all, wasn't a quota system,
with limited government funds going only to those balanced
books which could boast (on their sides like cereal boxes)
one latino, one woman, and one black. The hint, from every
quarter on campus, was that the professors chose their books
not for aesthetic reasons but because they were specifically
formulated to inculcate a worldview beneficial to U.S.
capitalism. Everything was relative.

"But everything isn't relative," Ross complained. They
were at lunch, Ross and Mark plus Peter. Peter's eyes
flashed—he was back in his old role, making challenging
statements to keep them thinking. At these meals, where
Ross and Mark went hoping to get information on Tom's

moods, they ended up reading and discussing the school paper. There was a special series on the Women's Studies program. It had lately split into two factions. The Women of Color felt they weren't being covered enough by "white" Women's Studies. Within the Women of Color program, Asian students felt they weren't getting enough air time. An Asian student went on, "I've talked with Asians from the East Coast, and their experience is one hundred and eighty degrees different from mine." Would, Ross wondered, things split along city lines too? The Asian experience downtown was far removed from the Asian experience uptown. The West 81st Street Asian Experience as opposed to the West 82nd Street one. "It's ridiculous," Ross said. "Eventually, people will just come here and study their own dossiers. They'll write theses called 'Things I Like, Things I Don't Like.' "

"Still," Peter said, shifting in his chair, "you can't say nothing is relative. Take this thing with you guys and Tom, for example. You go to the dean. He gets your side of the story. Now the odds are, that version would be completely different from Tom's. And who's to say which of you is right, and which is wrong? That's what I mean by relative."

Mark made a disgusted sound through his teeth. The term had brought out an angry, compressed side of him; he knew what was going on on campus couldn't be right, but he felt, with a helpless judiciousness, that he didn't have enough facts yet to make a decision. His eyes bulged with the force of things unsaid, like steam rattling the top of a kettle. On the hall, Tom began saying "Faggots" and "Assholes" each time he passed their doors. Ross couldn't stand sitting in his room. But when he walked the campus, he couldn't help thinking that these people, if their problem went public, would all have taken Tom's side. In a vote, it would be him

101

and Mark, and not Tom, who were expelled from Brown. What had seemed like a clear situation—Mark and Ross hadn't liked Tom—now seemed different; they'd disliked Tom not because of himself, but because of a complex system of codes imposed from the outside.

Ross began avoiding the campus entirely, going to parties off-campus. He'd bring Mark and Peter, then manage to get separated. He met a girl, Cynthia Dapney, at a party given by Cheryl Cohen, a girl from Dalton. He began spending weekends at Cynthia's house. She was a pretty, impeccably well dressed girl from Richmond, Virginia. She was wealthy, and she owned a car. Ross liked her. But instead of rejecting the ideas of the other students, Cynthia was in fact in favor of them. She'd become, since her arrival at Brown, deeply feminist. She showed Ross papers from her courses, dealing with "castration of women" and "political empowerment as a creator of meaning." Her friends were the semioticians, thin, exquisitely unhappy-looking women with prematurely drawn faces, as if the rigors of their discipline—having been exposed, at such a young age, to the evil clockwork levers and gears behind the seemingly benevolent face of the world—had sucked all the life out of them. Ross liked Cynthia, but the conflict, her believing in theory, his rejecting it, soon became unbearable. Even the word *theory* would make Ross cringe, with its smug refusal to be a theory about any particular thing at all.

At dinner—where Ross would have liked to tell Cynthia about Tom, ask her opinion about what to do, only he was afraid she'd gasp, "You mean, you wouldn't let him watch the football game?" and then Tom would jump out from beneath the table and begin pounding Ross's head in with the French bread—she would describe her courses, where everything was theorized. Novels, films, gender, all were forced to own up to their cultural preconceptions. Gays complained of the West's compulsory heterosexuality; Marxists pointed out the commercial imperatives implicit in everything, even in relations between men and women. Whenever Ross challenged these ideas, Cynthia would, with precise, chopping motions of her hands (sometimes tucking some hair behind an ear), aggressively defend them, as if to always assert the primacy of theory over life. She'd say, "You don't understand," which meant "You don't agree." But how could Cynthia agree with these things, with Ross lying naked beside her, his sweat still drying on her chest?

Cynthia had early-morning classes, and when she left for them Ross would get out of bed and, naked, flip through the books on her bookshelf. Many argued that women had been corrupted by men's language. One, by a French feminist psychoanalyst, asserted that all heterosexual sex was rape, "a violent break-in, a brutal disruption of the hegemony of the twin vaginal lips by the violating penis." Ross began to wonder about the healthiness of Cynthia's sexuality. He saw himself as a considerate lover. Did Cynthia feel violated by him? "No," she assured him, patting his arm, "you're my female imaginary." What did this mean?

The spring brought with it a final snowstorm, followed by a flurry of meetings. The Coalition for a Free South Africa held a fast, urging the Brown Corporation to rid itself of holdings in South Africa. Of the various groups on campus, Ross had come to hate the divestors most of all. One morning, he'd seen twenty or thirty of them shouting at the doddering, clearly frightened members of the corporation as they came slowly out of their quarterly meeting. When one of the corporation members walked back to the protestors, took off his hat, and tried to explain his position, the protestors began to chant, "Shut-up, Shut-up, Shut-up." It had nothing to do with politics—it was youth taunting age. When Ross stopped to consider it, the fast was a brave act; four students, twelve days, no food at all. But Ross refused to consider it. It would have been all right, if things on the hall hadn't been so bad. But they were getting worse by the day. Ross would be reading in his room and hear zinging and banging sounds from Mark's door. Stepping outside, he'd see Tom running into 216, a wrist rocket dangling from his arm. On Mark's door would be penny-sized nicks, and all around his doorway would be glowing pennies, as if from a slit money bag. He'd hear thumping against his own door, and in the hall would find round gray pebbles. His door, pockmarked, began to look like the inside of a beaten copper bowl. He was afraid he'd open it at the wrong moment and get hit by a rock in the face. He came back from class and found charred black rings on the bottom of the wood, along with the festive, pastel-colored papers that usually cover firecrackers. He was reading *Bleak House,* and looked out the window to see Tom kneeling on his fire escape, peering in. Plus, as if oddly in sync with Ross, Tom had acquired a girlfriend, a small, stringy sophomore (less pretty than Cynthia, Ross was happy to note) who accompanied Tom everywhere and who left their door open during sex, inviting the rest of the hall to listen in on the raptures to which Tom was transporting her. Ross and Mark took Peter to dinner every other night. What was Tom up to? Had he talked about hurting either of them? Peter laughed, fending off their questions with his hands.

"God, you guys take everything so seriously. He's just trying to get a rise out of you, that's all."

"Can't you tell him to cut it out?" Mark asked.

"I don't control Tom," Peter said, soberly. Perhaps it was part of being provocative, but more and more often in their conversations Peter took on the role of Tom's defender. "And if you think Tom's so dangerous, and violent, why don't you just go to your friend the dean and have him kicked out? He sounds like a menace to me."

"We could have, you know," Ross said. "That's what the dean wanted us to do. When we first went there, he asked if we wanted Tom out. Quote-unquote. And we said no, because we didn't want to get Tom in trouble. We just want him to stop bothering us."

"Well, I guess you made the wrong choice." When they didn't laugh, Peter said, "Okay, look, relax. I didn't see how nice you guys had been about letting Tom stay in your school. I hadn't realized what concerned guys you've been."

Mark made his disgusted noise again. That night, as Ross was undressing for bed, he heard Tom and Peter talking in the hall. He opened his door a crack and listened. Peter was saying, "And then Tifton started talking about how crazy he thought you were."

"He said that?" Tom rumbled, in an amazed voice.

Peter chuckled. "Yeah. He practically said he wanted to get you kicked out, but the dean wouldn't let him." Ross closed his door. Everything they'd said all year had gone straight to Tom. It didn't surprise him. When he told Mark about it, though, Mark was angry. Ross tried to explain that, when the hall split, Peter had been in a tight spot. Playing the two sides against each other had been the one way he could keep getting dinner invitations. Ross tried to get Mark to promise not to mention anything to him, but Mark said, "I can't promise anything." There was no question about it; Mark wasn't bright. But Ross was stuck with him. He'd dragged him into this situation. Indeed, Mark was his only friend at the school. He couldn't even bring Cynthia to his room, for fear that Tom would launch into something. He didn't feel at home anywhere. He went into the bathroom and there were lima beans floating in the oval reservoir of the toilet. He no longer had the sense of skimming over his life; he'd veered off, somehow, been carried away by a bad wind. He thought about the life he could have led—dinner once or twice a week with a friendly Tom, with freedom otherwise to carry out his social endeavors—and it seemed a paradise he'd insolently rejected. Every move away from Tom had, perversely, only brought them closer together, like Br'er Rabbit and the Tar Baby. The situation with Tom stuck to him, surrounded him. Ross and Mark were the soccer players in Tom's poster, stuck on a cliff, with their ball, the things they'd wanted, floating in the water hopelessly out of reach.

As March ended, and as the snow piles invisibly melted, two seniors were arrested for prostitution. Women's groups protested the *Herald*'s decision to print the names of the students involved. To the Sarah Doyle Research Center, the issue was simply an extension of the male-dominated capitalist ethic refusing to allow women control over their own bodies. Demonstrations were organized in support of the two girls. Cynthia attended. She felt that literature was too male-oriented, and she'd given it up. "Perhaps," she told Ross (this was the last time he saw her), "women need to move into the political sphere to take the appropriate action." She referred to literature as "the male canon of literature," as if it were yet another all-male club women would have to sue to be granted inclusion into. The demonstration became a fair celebrating all women; groups laid out huge white sheets over the Green, inviting other women to help decorate them with slogans and drawings. All over these sheets, the words *Women* and *Woman* were cleverly misspelled (*Womyn* was the most popular version) to avoid any reference to males. Through it all, no one discussed whether the girls were right or wrong to have been involved in prostitution, whether prostitution should or shouldn't be illegal. It was all relative. Who had made the legal system, after all, if not men? Ross began to wonder if maybe relativity itself wasn't relative, if only certain things were relative, and then only at certain times.

A letter arrived from John Erhenkrantz, happy in London. Ross imagined him, his perfect nose slicing through the English fog. At the close, John said, "Tell Peter to keep Tom in line." It was so inappropriate it was depressing; John was writing into a situation that no longer existed, like light coming from a dead star. Back on the hall, Mark was smiling guiltily, like a pet who has finally, by God, opened up the refrigerator and eaten all the people food in sight. "I couldn't help it," he said. "I told Peter we knew." Ross didn't say anything. "At first, he didn't understand why I was so upset, but then he started saying how he had to be loyal to Tom. I told him he couldn't keep sitting on the fence. Then I asked why he'd lied about what we'd said, and he said he wasn't going to talk to me if I was going to keep shouting, and then he left my room." Mark grinned again. "So I guess that's it, huh?" Ross thought that at least now he didn't have to feel responsible anymore; whatever happened would be at least partially Mark's fault.

It was a good thing spring break came then, for it wasn't clear how much longer things could have lasted on the hall. Ross left Brown on Wednesday. Thursday afternoon Mark called him at home. He had come back from class, and there was a huge sheet of paper hanging on the dorm wall, with a line drawn down the middle. On one side it said, "Hatfields," and on the other it said, "McCoys." Ross said he didn't even want to think about it till he came back. This proved impossible, though, and Ross spent the entire vacation thinking about Tom Creely. Easter was the holiday the Tiftons went away. This year they went to Tryall, in Jamaica. It rained every day they were there. Ross's father hung around with a group of businessmen, driving in carts over the golf course, disembarking to hit a ball, then hopping back in and bouncing over the spongy green to the next tee. Ross's mother traveled the island looking at Caribbean art. Ross didn't want to do either. He sat in his room reading, or else hung around the bar of the hotel. Through the windows, the soaked palms looked like soggy tarantulas perching on concrete pillars. Ross drank coffee and vaguely watched pretty high school girls talking to boys the same age. The boys had longish hair and funny, floral bathing suits, and seemed relaxed and stylish in a way that Ross wasn't. You were probably never cooler in your whole life than you were your last year in high school, Ross realized. He was so depressed that by mid-week his mother, returning from one of her sorties laden with canvases, asked what was going on. The whole thing just came out then. Mrs. Tifton was horrified. She touched her chin and said, "You always do attract the lunatics, don't you?" The family discussed Tom over dinner, and Ross was sorry he'd let it slip out. Creely had followed him even to Jamaica; there was no escape from him anywhere. Ross said, "Look, let's not get overly excited about this. In four more weeks the term will be over, and I'll never have to see Tom Creely again."

"In just four weeks he managed to beat up you and your friend, isn't that right?" Mrs. Tifton asked, snappily. Even in the cloudy weather, she'd managed to develop the necessary tan; when her eyes narrowed, their sides showed veins of white. "I don't want to have to think about your life being at risk for four more weeks."

"Oh, Mom. My life isn't at risk."

Ross got off lightly, with his mother making him promise to see the dean right when he got back to school. But the vacation was ruined, and at least twice a day his mother would ask him, her voice going up a notch, for further details about life on the hall, or for clarification of points already described. When he returned to Providence and saw Mark, Ross could tell from a certain harried, exhausted expression that Mark had had similar conversations with his own parents. They saw Dean Sackler first thing Monday morning, told him what had happened since February. The dean—sitting across from them, his forearms resting on the blotter of his desk—listened with a measuring expression, as if he were plugging their information into a special dean formula which, when all the integers were entered, would then produce their solution. Mark said, "I think the problem is that nobody's ever told Tom the way he acts is wrong." Mark's conflict with Peter had given him a new boldness, and he seemed bent on exercising his new partial ownership of the situation. Dean Sackler cocked his head. This was information that did not fit into his formula, and he was trying to let it slide gently out of his ear.

"It seems to me we have a number of options here," he said. He counted them off on his fingers. "One, we send Tom home now. Frankly, I'm about ready to throw up my hands and do that right now, if you two want it. Do you?" He looked at them sharply. When neither responded, he went on, "Two, you say there've been wrist rockets and firecrackers. Both those items are in direct violation of the code of student conduct. I'd like to search Creely's room, with Brown Security. If we came up with anything, Tom's expulsion would become a university matter, totally out of our hands. How does that sound to you?"

Ross liked the idea of not having to decide about Tom, but

he was nervous about having Tom's room searched. Mark was too. It seemed to be pushing things. Dean Sackler shrugged. Maybe what they should do, he said, was go back to their rooms. If things had cooled off, fine. But if not, at the first sign of trouble, all they'd have to do was call him up and he could get the whole Brown Security process going in an afternoon. He stood up. His solution had been delivered, and Ross and Mark found themselves first on the Green, where a line of students was moving in and out of Wilson Hall, and then back in their rooms, on Miller Hall.

The hall had changed again. The poster Mark had described was gone, having been removed by the custodial staff over the vacation. One of the fluorescent bulbs had burned out, giving the hall an oppressive, brooding quality, like a man with half-lidded eyes. Ross went in and out of his room quickly, hoping to avoid any chance meetings with Tom or Peter. Things were quiet, and Ross thought that perhaps this vacation, as all the others had failed to, had soothed Tom. Tuesday, Tom wasn't in class, but Wednesday he was. Afterwards, as Ross was walking to the library, Tom loomed up before him from nowhere. Ross flinched, but Tom just clapped him on the back, said, "Have a nice day, buddy. See you around," and kept on walking. Back at the dorm, Mark had found a note under his door: "Hope this makes up for everything. Friends for life, Tom." Included with the note was a coupon for a dozen free Dunkin' Donuts. "Maybe things have calmed down," Mark said to Ross. He looked at the back of the coupon which, while undoubtedly generous, was still good only at participating stores. Ross felt immensely relieved. Raiding Tom's room would have been completely unnecessary. It seemed the one wrong turn he hadn't taken all year. It was the same feeling he got in New York, when he missed the express and took the local and then, shuttling along down the dark tunnel, saw the express sitting stalled on the tracks.

That night, after eleven-thirty, it was as if a troupe of witches and warlocks had been loosed on the hall. Ross was awakened by pounding on his door. "Open up, Tifton!" Tom said. Ross didn't do anything. Tom kept banging on his door, and then he and Peter went running up and down the hall, making the most noise possible, slapping the walls as they went. They walked across the way and pounded on Mark's door for a while. "What are you doing on that fence, Peter?" Tom said. "I don't know," Peter said, "but I can't get off. The fence is where all us awful people sit." Peter had completely gone over to the other side. Ross heard banging sounds on his own door, followed by the rubbery zing of the wrist rocket. Tom sang his "Mr. Classic" song. His girlfriend came loudly, a series of short, gasping breaths followed by a long final one, a woman giving birth to an immense, relieved sigh. She was faking it, to annoy them. Tom and Peter kept slapping the walls. Tom said, "I'm going to get me a shotgun, handle this little Tifton problem once and for all." It was frightening but, in a way, liberating; Tom had taken their difficult decision out of their hands. Ross got out of bed, locked his window. He was awakened a few hours later by someone shaking his door. "Ross! Are we roommates, Ross?"

In the morning, they of course called the dean. Dean Sackler's voice was rapid-fire, happy; he was getting his chance to be a bulldog. Brown Security would be there to search Tom's room Friday morning at eight-thirty. At eight o'clock, Mark knocked on Ross's door, looking serious and not speaking, his hair disheveled from sleep. He had a textbook in his hand. They tried reading for a while. By eight twenty-five, Mark was pacing the room. "They're probably raiding some other room by mistake right now," he said. A few seconds later they heard the hall door open, then footsteps, accompanied by the jangle of keys and the staccato, extra-sharp sound of voices on a walkie-talkie. Mark turned to Ross with his finger over his mouth, meaning he wanted to listen in.

Dean Sackler called them an hour later, to tell what had happened. He'd gone into Tom's room with Security. Tom was there, with his girlfriend. They waited until the girlfriend left, and then Dean Sackler asked if Tom had any firecrackers. Tom said he didn't know what the dean was talking about. Dean Sackler said that if they found the firecrackers on their own, it would just be worse. Tom said he still didn't know what the dean was talking about. So Security searched. They found three firecrackers right on top of Tom's desk. Dean Sackler asked if there were any more, and Tom said "Nope" again, though when they went through his dresser they found almost a full pack under some T-shirts. Then the dean asked about the wrist rocket. Tom said he didn't have a wrist rocket. "I told him he was making a mistake," the dean said. They found the wrist rocket hanging in his closet. They'd taken him down to the Brown Security office, where he was making a statement. Hearing these things, Ross swelled with guilty elation; he pictured Tom in handcuffs—though he knew Brown didn't use handcuffs—being fingerprinted in a police station. Things were finally out of their hands; it was official, Tom was going to be sent home. The dean paused with a contented sigh, as if merely retelling the episode had brought back its pleasant exhaustion.

"Here's what we're going to do," Dean Sackler said. "You boys get showered, have breakfast. I'll walk over to Security and pick up Tom's statement. I want you back in my office at twelve for a quick meeting. I'll try to get Tom and Peter in here, and then the five of us can have a group conference, see if we can't all finally get this business sorted out."

"But I thought we were having Tom sent home," Ross said.

"We can still do that," Dean Sackler said. "Sure. I just thought we'd try to talk it out now, with Tom knowing we have these things over him, before you and Mark decide. Fair enough?"

It was. Mark went back to his own room. Ross picked up his book. He wanted to finish *In Our Time*, which he had to write an in-class paper on the following week (sexism and racism were the recommended topics, the recommended story "The Battler"). In-class papers were the newest fad at Brown—essentially, they were exams with a single essay question. After a little while, Ross got up to brush his teeth. In the hallway, Tom walked right by him. Ross was stunned. Tom was wearing his towel, and his head and upper body were soaking. He stared at Ross with a compressed, reprisal-promising expression. Ross ran into Mark's room, dragged him up to the bathroom, then pointed out the shower head, which was still dripping. "Look at that," he said. "Guess who's here? Tom just took a shower." There was no one in the bathroom but the Egyptian boy, who was standing at the sink washing a chicken. He had one hand in the cavity—like a grotesque mitten—and was rotating the bird under the water. "Good morning," the Egyptian said, placidly. Ross had a terrible thought that, in the eyes of this boy, there was no difference between him and Mark and Tom and Peter. They were all the same, equally engaged in some noisy, unfathomable American collegiate custom.

"What are you talking about?" Mark said.

"Tom's here, back on the hall, right now. He was just using the shower."

The Egyptian boy removed his arm from the chicken. In

his hand he was clutching the purple, paper-wrapped inner organs, which he stacked on the shelf in front of the mirror. Ross took Mark into the hall. There was Tom, talking to Peter in front of Peter's door. "It's great," Peter was saying. "Finally, somebody's going to have to listen to your side of the story."

Ross and Mark ran over to the dean's office. Dean Sackler was wearing a suit, in preparation for their conference, and was watering his plants. Ross was surprised they needed watering; he'd thought they grew by themselves, on a steady diet of strong advice and their own solid work habits. Mark sat down and announced that he refused to go back to the dorm while Tom was still there. "What's the point of all this?" he asked. "I thought you were sending Creely home." The dean shrugged. "He asked if he could use the shower. I didn't see who it could hurt, frankly." Ross, too, felt betrayed. They sat in his office until a quarter of twelve. Then Dean Sackler phoned his secretary. "Are Tom Creely and Peter Abrahms here yet? Well, you might as well send them in now, I've got Mark Caron and Ross Tifton already in my office."

Tom and Peter walked in together. To Ross's astonishment, they were both wearing ties, slacks, and blazers. For the first time since Ross had known him, Tom had a clean shave; Peter, with his darting eyes, looked like the crooked lawyer of an already convicted congressman. They sat down at the same time, as if choreographed. The dean leaned against the edge of his desk. As he began to speak, Peter raised his hand, holding a finger up at shoulder level.

"Before anything gets started here," he said, "I'd like to request that another dean be brought in on this. We're not saying we don't trust you, Dean Sackler—"

"Wait a second," Dean Sackler said. "You're Peter Abrahms, right?"

"Yes." The dean leaned forward and they shook hands, glancingly, fingers-to-fingers instead of palm-to-palm. Peter took a breath and put his hand back up, as if it were an integral part of his speech process (the way you flip the lever up on a self-serve gas pump, Ross thought). He slid back into his official voice, which was a half octave deeper and a lot smoother than his regular one. "Now, what I'm saying is that it's not that we don't trust you, Dean Sackler. But we are worried that you're a little prejudiced on this thing. You've been hearing from Ross and Mark about this all year—"

"Actually," the dean said, "this is just the third time they've been in my office."

Peter's eyes did their dazzling scan of Dean Sackler's face as the dean spoke. Ross thought he'd never hated anyone more than he hated Peter at that moment. Peter resumed, "What Tom feels is that nobody has ever tried to listen to his side of this thing. You've been hearing Ross and Mark whine about him, and our feeling is that you just can't see straight anymore about what's really been happening on this hall. That's just human. I mean, if I'd only heard one side of a story, I'd be predisposed to believe only that point of view, too. What we'd like is for you to bring another dean in on this. Otherwise, this whole discussion isn't worth anything, and there's no reason for Tom to come in and defend himself. We can just go back to the dorm and Mark and Ross can complain about us all they want."

Ross looked at Peter; Peter returned his look for a second with a faint smile, then looked humbly down, like a basketball player after making a difficult shot, running to get back on defense. Ross could clearly see how things were going to go. Mark was staring at Ross aghast. Dean Sackler thought for a moment, then said, "That sounds fair enough." He stood up straight and called his secretary again. He asked her to find out what Dean White's schedule looked like for the rest of the afternoon. Would he be available for a student conference around, say, twelve-thirty? Peter whispered something to Tom, who nodded, snorting at the truth of whatever Peter had said. Ross looked out the window. It seemed odd, suddenly, that all those students could be going about their business, moving in and out of buildings, without any idea as to what was happening in the dean's office. Dean Sackler nodded again. Then he hung up and said, "That was Dean White. He's going to meet with us here at one o'clock. Is that okay?"

There wasn't time, in the half hour between meetings, to go back to Miller and get showered, so Ross and Mark took a walk off campus. Neither of them spoke. They walked down George Street, then up along Benefit, past the sturdy, historic houses, many of which had plaques by their doors, saying who'd built them and what year they'd been built. It was sunny, and hot. The shadows of leaves made fine decorations on the sidewalk, and the smell of the many flowering plants was intoxicating. The dogwoods were back in bloom, dousing parked cars with petals. It made Ross think of the first day he'd arrived; it would have been hard to imagine, then, that the opening cone of his life could have so inverted as to narrow him to this point. They turned on Prospect Street and walked up the steep incline until they came to the small park at the top of the hill. It was called Overlook by the students, because it was built onto a terrace that overlooked the entire city. You could see all of Providence from it: the four skyscrapers which marked the business district, the trains chugging in and out of Union Station, the flags snapping crisply on top of the state house. In the middle of this park was a statue of Roger Williams, Rhode Island's founder, in that 1930s' style, WPA, which makes everyone look like a foreman in a Soviet machine shop. The statue had been set forward on the terrace, behind a black fence composed of upraised arrows and black bands, so that Williams, too, could look out over the city. His pose was an uncertain one, as if he were actually viewing Providence and it was surprising him.

Ross and Mark stepped over the fence and stood next to the statue. Mark took a deep breath, as if to speak. Ross could see Mark's eyes dilating as they focused on what his words would be. Then Ross started talking. It felt good to talk. In a story he'd read as a boy, all the winds of the world were stored up in a single cave, released only on special occasions. This was how Ross's voice felt to Ross now. Words exploded from him. "God damn it," he said. "Don't you see? This is the whole problem. Everyone thinks there are two sides to everything. That you can explain anything. That if you have explanations, everything is better. But if that's true, then it doesn't matter who behaves the best; it only matters who explains their actions the best. Don't you see what's going to happen? Tom's going to explain to Dean Sackler how he felt we didn't pay enough attention to him. Then the dean is going to nod and say it was everyone's fault. Is that the year we've had on this hall? Are we all going to shake hands or something? What do you think? Mark?"

Mark said, "I don't know."

Ross kept talking. It was as if both sides of him were constricting, and the only relief possible was to keep talking, to construct a rope of words to climb out on. "We have a chance to say to Tom, this is right, this is wrong. No explanations, no second stories, nothing. Peter's going to sit there explaining what Tom's motivations were all year, why he beat us up, why he shot rocks at our doors, and the dean is going to listen and say he didn't have the whole story. Is that the whole story? This guy tortured us for two terms. There is no other side to this thing. We ask him, Tom, are these firecrackers yours? Is this wrist rocket yours? And then we expel him. Simple as that. We can't let Peter twist it around. We can't let Tom and Peter walk off thinking they did the right thing. We have to go back into that office and say this isn't just relative values, that someone did the wrong thing, and we can show it."

And then Ross was finished. The cave had shut. Mark was looking at him. Ross took a deep breath and looked out over the city. A train was pulling out of Union Station—Ross imagined the people on it, looking disinterestedly out the scratchy windows—and a church bell rang somewhere close by, marking the hour. "We should probably be getting back," Mark said.

Dean White, it turned out, was black; a small, handsome man in a brown jacket and flannel slacks, which he hitched up before sitting down. Dean Sackler gave him a quick rundown of the situation. Peter broke in at various places, pointing out descriptions that were biased or unfair. As Dean Sackler spoke, Dean White looked at the four of them, and it occurred to Ross that to him it was Ross and Mark—who hadn't even showered—and not Tom and Peter who looked grungy and unwholesome. Dean White even pointed at Ross and asked, "You're—Tom?" before Dean Sackler cleared up the mistake.

Ross looked out the window. Dean Sackler began asking questions. What had happened? Why couldn't they get along? Did they think they could get along now? Ross answered. Dean Sackler, he saw, had no real interest in having things work out correctly. He just wanted them to work out with the minimum fuss possible, so that no one person would be any more unhappy than anyone else. And truthfully, Ross had spent all his passion yelling at the Overlook. There wasn't really any reason to do anything. He'd said what he wanted to say, now he just wanted to get off the hall. Peter kept talking, twisting things—his hands, shaping complicated points in the air, seemed to be actually twisting his words as they fluttered out—and even Mark didn't seem upset anymore. Things were out of their hands. Dean Sackler asked everyone if they thought they could manage to live together for three more weeks. They all nodded. "Ross?" the dean asked. Ross nodded again. It was going to be written down as everyone's fault. Afterwards, Ross and Mark shook hands with the dean in his office. He had a relieved air, like a musician after a performance, revealing places he'd almost slipped up. If he'd smoked, he would have lit a cigarette. "Are you two satisfied?" he asked. "Because I'm still ready to send Tom home right now, if the two of you want it."

Ross said, "No. You're right. It's only about twenty-two days. I'm sure we can all handle it."

The dean nodded, smiling merrily, and said, "Well, I told you things would work out." He walked them to the door and closed it behind them. Ross worked for the three weeks, finishing up his courses. The hall was quiet. Peter passed by with a triumphant smirk each time he saw them. Tom disappeared from Ross's classes. Ross thought how nice it would have been if he'd dropped them entirely, but no, on the last day, there was Tom, sitting hunched over at a desk by the door. As Ross walked by he nodded, which was a kind of farewell. Ross took his exams, handed in his papers, shook Mark's hand, and went home for the summer.

ANSWERS

THE MACHINE SNAPS ON right when the phone rings, and I hear my mother's voice, on tape, saying she isn't here. Her voice always sounds different from real life on the tape, either too vivacious (like she's calling in from the middle of a party, one finger stoppering her ear) or else too solemn. I wait. After the beep, my mother starts talking in real life, street noises behind her.

"Richard? It's eleven-thirty. I'm going to Gristede's—"

I pick up the phone. "Mom?" I say. I have the receiver too close to the machine, and there's feedback; I step back, the whining stops. On the machine, my voice sounds breathless.

"You're home?" my mother asks, in an amused voice.

"The machine got to it first," I say. This isn't exactly a lie.

My mother laughs. Hearing her on both the phone and in the machine is interesting, like stereo. A rumbling goes past her, right through our living room. "You're weird," she says.

Every time I don't answer the phone my mother makes believe that she doesn't know why. But she does know why. I just moved in, after three years of living in Los Angeles with my father. The thing is, I haven't officially told him yet.

I was spending the summer with my mom on Cape Cod, and was due back in California last week, to begin getting ready for the ninth grade. I didn't go. My mother called my father for me. He refused to listen to her, and since then, I've been waiting for him to call me here. When my mother goes jogging, or to the store, or to her studio, I turn the machine on and listen in.

This upsets my mother for two reasons. She wants me to answer the phone like a normal person. And if not, she wants me to at least admit that the reason why is that I'm afraid of my father. I could easily *say* that, but it isn't really the truth. For some reason, it's become extremely important to me, in the last few weeks, not to say anything that isn't at least partially true—like saying the machine picked up before I did.

I put my sneakers on and walk over to the supermarket. It's cool in there. At this hour, the only people in Gristede's are elderly, sweatered women—even now, in 85-degree weather, they're dressed for January—and their Jamaican maids. It takes a while to find my mother. I don't want to go around yelling "Mom," so I kind of say it, in a soft voice, as I pass each aisle. She's in the bread and cereal section, putting some bran flakes into the cart. I take them out and drop in two boxes of Quaker 100% Natural instead.

My mother gestures at the cereal. "That's why I wanted you to come," she says, in an aggrieved way. "I don't know what you like, yet."

"Here I am," I say. In California, I always ate Quaker. I liked to put it in a mug and pop it, dry, into my mouth while I watched television. In fact, this is probably what I would be doing if I were back in L.A. getting ready for ninth grade right now.

My mother and I push our cart down the aisle, past the pasta, towards the dairy case. Everything hums here, as if there are ghosts in the milk cartons. My mom says, "You know, you're going to have to start answering the phone eventually. You can't just stay holed up in the house not answering, like a fugitive."

"I was in the bathtub," I say. Yesterday, I think.

"Oh," my mother says. She laughs through her nose, as if snorting this explanation away.

When my dad and I moved away, my mother started seeing a therapist. This therapist, I know, has instructed her not to push me on this issue. "When you're ready to talk about this," she told me this weekend, "I'll be right here." Neither she nor her therapist realized, of course, that this was a form of pushing, too. I didn't clue them in.

In the meat section, where continent-shaped cuts sit stacked neatly in Styrofoam and cellophane, Mom sorts through for a reasonably fresh package, then drops some lamb chops into our cart. I reach in and take them out, picking up a package of hamburger meat instead. "I don't like lamb," I say.

My mother looks at the lamb mournfully. "It was on sale," she says.

"So? Just because something's on sale doesn't mean it's good. If I don't like eating it, how have we saved money? You're supposed to like what you eat."

On the checkout line, my mother says, "It's just that I get a lot of business calls, Richard, and most people don't like talking to a machine."

"If I was in Los Angeles, the machine would answer anyway."

This is true, but it isn't a nice thing to say. My mother purses her lips. Two elderly women are in front of us, one of them buttoning up a pink cardigan. As the girl tallies up their purchases, they keep looking at the register, asking, "What was two eighty-seven?" or, "Didn't you already ring

2

those peas?" The checkout girl handles this very good-naturedly, smiling. She's probably used to it. They probably have a special training course at Gristede's: Handling the West 72nd Street Crowd. I pick up a copy of *People* and read the movie reviews. When our turn comes, I put it back on the rack. My mother is looking at me.

"Do you want me to buy that for you?" she asks.

I shake my head. "It's not on sale."

At home, we have lunch and then spend two hours going over the Stuyvesant test. Stuyvesant is a special public school: you have to pass a long, multiple-choice test to get in. "We can't afford for you to go to private school," my mother says, "though I'd love to send you." I shrug. I've always been good at these exams, so I'm not worried. The book we practice from is a big Barron's book, full of old Stuyvesant tests, answers explained in the back. We've taken most of the exams before, and I don't tell my mom, as I take the test, that I've memorized a good number of the answers. We go over the ones I've missed. In the back are the ghosts of all our previous goings-over, long sketchy lists—my mom's handwriting, mine—of diminishing remainders and fractions. The test is on Wednesday—two days from now. If I get in, I'll be a Stuyvesant student next Monday. Neither of us knows, I don't think, what will happen if I don't pass this test.

After we've gone over everything the phone rings. My mother looks at me expectantly. "Aren't you going to get it?" I ask, my voice rising.

"I'm tired from jogging," she says, folding her arms over the Barron's book in her lap. "Can't you get it?"

"I have to get a drink of water." I stand. The phone keeps ringing. "Well?" I say. "It could be a business call."

My mother sighs and gets up. I go into the kitchen. My mother answers in the living room. Whenever my dad calls, her voice gets very pinched and artificial, so I can tell, listening, that it's not him. I go into the bedroom and switch on the television set. My mother comes in. She sits down next to me and turns off the volume.

"I was thinking of going to my studio for a while, if you don't mind." She puts her hand on top of my head, a sort of crown.

"That's fine," I say. "Maybe I'll do a few more practices in the Stuy book."

My mother smiles. "We could go over the answers at dinner," she says. I knew this would please her.

My mother is a sculptor, though she really makes her living teaching sculpture at Hunter College. When she and Dad were married, she was very popular. Then, when my dad and I went to California, she didn't do any work for more than a year. It's awful to think you could have that kind of effect on a person. Every time she goes to her studio now, I feel relieved. Her sculptures are made of garbage—"found objects" ("A Found Artist," said the *Art News* article about her, years ago, when she was big). She goes around the street picking up interesting things, then welds them onto slabs of bronze. In *Sunday, 1971,* for example, she had a broken shopping cart, running shoes, a jar of Gatorade, a blue paper Greek diner coffee cup, and the *Times* magazine section. It was strange, when I lived with her, to come home from school and find her hunting around our neighborhood for garbage. She looked like just another lunatic. Sometimes, people passing—tourists probably, since nobody in SoHo ever reacted to anything— would stop and offer her change. I used to ask why she didn't weld that into her sculptures too.

In the afternoon, the phone rings. I lower the volume on

the TV. After five rings, it's clear the machine isn't going to pick up. I go into the living room. Sure enough, the machine's off. I stand over the phone, listening to it, putting my hand on the black receiver. I can feel the ring in there, a vibration under my fingers, like a heartbeat. It's like I'm holding my father's head underwater.

Tuesday morning, Mom out jogging, I wake up hearing the machine. I'm in the bedroom. Since I came back, my mother has been sleeping on the futon in the living room. "A high school boy should have a bedroom," she said. I walk into her room in my underwear. Everyone in the opposite wing of the building can see me, but I can't imagine any of them getting that big a thrill out of a fourteen-year-old boy in his Jockeys. My grandmother is speaking. "Hello? Richard? Joan?"

I pick up the phone. "Grandma?" I say.

"Richard, why haven't you called your father?"

I turn the machine off—I don't want this being recorded. My grandmother lives in Florida. She used to live in Westchester. After my grandfather died, she moved down to the Fort Lauderdale condominium where all her Westchester friends were already living. They're all together now, in the same complex, like a transplanted ant colony. The only difference is that now the men wear golf caps, and the women cleats. It's weird, like one of those *Twilight Zone*s where everyone has a perfect double living a slightly altered life. I sit down on the windowsill, a few paint splinters rubbing against my bare legs. "Is he very angry?" I ask.

"He's hurt, Rich. When he got off the phone with Joan he told me he went for a walk around the block. He went walking around and around all night, trying to figure out what he'd done to upset you." This image, of my father orbiting our mock-Tudor house, is painfully vivid. My grandmother, with a good sense for the family theatric, gives it a minute to sink in. "Why *did* you move out, Richard?"

"It had nothing to do with Dad," I say. "Could you tell him that?"

"Why don't you tell him? He's very hurt that you haven't spoken to him. He's your father. You should call him yourself."

I take the Stuyvesant test Wednesday morning. It's supposed to start at ten and run till after lunch. So as not to risk any slip-ups (what if there's a fire on the tracks? for example) my mother decides we shouldn't take the subway. We take a cab instead. As we drive, she gives me my final instructions, like a coach. "Don't spend too much time on any question. If you have extra time, go back over your answers. Don't try to be the first one out of the room. Also, be careful with your answer sheet. You messed up on some of the practices. This exam is graded by machines, and you can't explain a mistake to a machine like you can to me. Be careful on long division."

I march into the exam armed with three number-two pencils, a fresh Pink Pearl eraser (a rubbery trapezoid, all corresponding angles equal), and two candy bars, a Snickers and a Reese's, for brainpower. The room is jam-packed. All the kids look nervous, anxious. We know that three-fourths of us aren't going to get in, and we look like the desperate passengers on a sinking ship, watching as everyone else loads into the lifeboats. The parents all wait outside, close-lipped, smoking. It's how I imagine husbands act in a maternity ward. As the clock moves towards ten, I begin to feel more and more light-headed. If I screw up, I tell myself, I'm going back to California. It seems absurd—unfair, somehow—that so much of life can come suddenly down to single moments.

But the exam, to my relief, is easy. I zip right through. The Barron's book has simply prepared me for a much more difficult test. Reading Comprehension—my best practice exam subject—is like a little vacation in the Alps. I have a habit, when I'm nervous, of too-easily laughing. The dead-end answers make me laugh out loud. The kids around glare at me. I apologize with my eyebrows, mouthing the word "sorry," but then a second later ("The author of this passage suggests that the best way to solve problems is to: e) drink beer") I am laughing again.

By twelve thirty-five, I've finished everything. I look up, cracking my back. I've been so involved in the exam, I haven't noticed where we are. We're in the school's library—there are posters saying "Reading—An Adventure," and things like that, showing an Indiana Jones figure being menaced by a cobra as he runs with some books under his arm, trying to avoid the fines, most likely. I look down at my place. I haven't used the Pink Pearl, though one of my pencil's erasers is solidly black with grease. I look at my answer sheet, at the black, filled-in ovals zigzagging their way down the page like a slaloming skier. My body sort of freezes. I only have 178 answers; there should be 180. The undersides of my arms tingle. How could I have made this mistake? I run down the answers. At 100 there is a space where I've answered two questions on the same line. Even though we're not allowed to, I open my booklet and go back. Then I begin erasing all my other answers and filling them back in. Thick pink dust from my eraser rolls all over the smooth finish, and the table shakes so much under my arm that the other kids' pencils shoot up and down over their own papers like seismographs. At 150 I find a question I missed entirely. It's math, long division. I complete it and check it as the proctor, walking past us, says, "Five minutes, please." I finish a minute after one o'clock, just after the "All pencils down" signal. As we begin piling our booklets, the proctor—a student, I can see, and by his tan probably just back from a summer at the beach—says, "That wasn't so bad, was it? See you in September."

We all walk out into the dark, anxious hallway. My mother is in the middle of the receiving line of parents. When I walk up to her, she quickly searches my face for signs of how it went. Then she asks, in as flat a voice as possible, "You make out okay?" She has a cigarette in her hand—something I haven't seen her with in a long while. Before I get a chance to answer, she lets the cigarette fall end over end to the floor, where it glows for a moment before she puts it out with her foot.

To celebrate, my mother takes me out to dinner and then a movie. She lets me pick the movie. There's nothing in the paper she'd even remotely like to see, so I take her to *Beverly Hills Cop II*. I point out the sights in California that I recognize, but after an hour I realize this is upsetting her, so I stop. On the walk home, across the park, she doesn't mention the film again—a sure sign she didn't enjoy it. As we come up to our building, I am struck with a plausible suspicion that Dad is going to be inside. He could easily have come: I imagine him on the plane, catching a cab at Kennedy, his shirt back wrinkled from sitting so long, then convincing the handyman at our building to let him in, showing with his driver's license how he has the same last name as we do. He and Mom will talk, then I'll be dragged back to California. I hang back as Mom opens the door, and when nothing special happens I walk warily in behind her.

My mom is sitting on the futon, the Barron's book in her lap. "Relieved?" she asks.

For a second, I think she means, Relieved Dad's not here? Then I realize she means the test. "I'm glad it's out of the way."

My mother nods, lifting her eyebrows. "I bet." She looks at the heavy book. "Well, we won't be needing this any-more." She tosses it onto the floor, where it goes *thunk*. "I just hope you got in," she says.

"It was pretty easy," I say.

"Knock wood," my mother says. Then, to my surprise, she reaches down and raps the cherry-wood frame under the futon. Twice. It's a shock to discover that my mother is superstitious, though I would have known it if I hadn't been in California for the last three years.

Next morning, during breakfast, the phone rings again. I have a pretty good idea who it is, and my mother does, too. She gets right up, with a steely face, and answers the phone. I spoon some knobby Quaker 100% Natural into my mouth. A second later, I hear my mother whoop in triumph. I've gotten into Stuyvesant. "I'm so relieved," my mother says. "I didn't know what we were going to do if you didn't make it." One of the nice things about my mother is that she never reveals how much was at stake in a given issue until after it's been resolved.

She takes me out for ice cream, but it's too hot to walk, even in the park. When I offer a squirrel the bottom of my sugar cone he stands there considering it, then seems to decide that, in the heat, it isn't worth running the few extra steps necessary to get the morsel. I toss it to him anyhow. We discuss school clothes and allowance. On the way home, my mother falls silent, thinking about something. We pass a big pile of garbage, and it pains me, for a moment, to think that if I wasn't here, if I were in Los Angeles, she would be sorting through it right now. I haven't told her how close I came to failing the test. She'd probably interpret it in some screwy way, no doubt, like that I didn't really want to come to New York after all.

In our apartment, my mother sits me down and says, "Look, I know you're afraid to talk to your father." She looks at my face. "Let's rationally discuss this. What's the worst thing he could do? Yell at you? I have an idea. You get on the phone in the bedroom. I'll get on in the living room. If your father starts getting abusive or threatening, I'll step in and you can get off the phone. Okay? There's nothing to be afraid of."

It sounds like a good idea. It's important for her to hear that I'm staying in the city from my own lips—as important as it is for my dad to hear it, though for the exact opposite reason. When she found out we were moving to Los Angeles, my mother threatened a lawsuit. She said that unless she was sure I wanted to go, she wasn't going to let us move. So I went over to her apartment—this apartment—one night and told her yes, I wanted to move. That was that.

Mom picks up the phone too early, while I'm still dialing, so that the phone company doesn't put the call through. We both hang up. I dial again, wait until I can hear, with a click and then static, that we're linked up with the long-distance network, and then I call my mother. "Mom!" I say. She picks up, another person jumping into this dark water near me. "I'm here," she says. I hear her covering the mouthpiece with her hand, a scrunchy sound, and then I'm aware of a kind of determined silence on her end of the line, a plugged opening, like the stop on a flute. In Los Angeles, the phone begins to ring.

"Hello?" my stepmother says.

"Lynn? It's Richard. Could you put my father on, please?"

There's a kind of scuffle on their end. My stepmother puts the phone down on the table. Through it, I can picture the whole kitchen, as if the receiver were a lens. The wood-finish cabinets, the green refrigerator with its notes and cartoons magnetically attached, the sink, the plants on the sill, the houses across the way. I hear my mother adjusting her palm for a more silent grip on the mouthpiece. I hear my father picking up, fitting the receiver against his cheek and lips in Los Angeles.

"Richard?" he says, in his slow, sad, telephone voice. And then I begin to cry. I imagine him walking around the block. I remember the year I lived with him in New York, before he married my stepmother, how, one night, when a friend of mine stayed over, he got us pizza ("You've tried the rest, now try the best," the box, like all pizza boxes in New York, said). I kept waiting to get used to Los Angeles, but I never did. I felt like a kid who gets assigned to the wrong class due to a programming error, and then sits in on the first few periods anyway, waiting for the error to be discovered so he can be moved. One night in Los Angeles, while we were driving through gleaming Century City to Ralph's Super-market, my father looked over at me, as I was changing the radio station (I'd heard Steely Dan in another car, and was trying to find it). "You can't know what a pleasure it's been, Richard," he said, "watching you grow up." I kept thinking how my mother wasn't having that pleasure. Now, he isn't going to have it. I think about how nice it would be to live in a world like the one my grandmother and her friends inhabited, where a version of you could live in New York and an exact replica could live in California. I hear my mother hanging up, in the living room, a click on the line.

"Richard?" my father asks, thinking the click is me. "Are you still there?" My mother is standing in the doorway, a surprised, complex expression on her face.

"I haven't hung up," I say into the phone. "I'm still here."

COLONISTS

TALL, SLIGHTLY SOUTHERN-VOICED, in a dark linen shirt buttoned all the way to the neck and silver, round-framed glasses, Mark Bell asks, "Ellen, how's the work coming?"

Answering, Ellen cocks her head and runs a hand through her dark hair. She has been celibate, deliberately celibate, for six weeks. All through dinner she has been watching Mark Bell, trying to decide whether or not she should sleep with him. As he sliced and forked his meat, not talking until he'd finished chewing, or at least had gotten a morsel tucked invisibly back into his mouth, Ellen had thought, Yes. As he laughed excessively at what she considered a pretty stupid story about New Hampshire residents, Ellen decided, No. As he took too big a forkful of salad and, finding squiggly alfalfa sprouts and oily loops of onion hanging from his lips, had simply stuffed the food into his mouth rather than making a joke or big deal out of it, Ellen decided "Yes" again. Salad has always been a difficult food for Ellen, too.

At their table with them are a hawk-nosed woman writing a novel about a female rabbi and a kindly, round-faced priest working out a series of erotic love poems so explicit that, when Ellen heard them in a reading at the colony library, they made her hair stand on end. These two are oblivious to the charge at their table, which has persisted through Ellen's shufflings and reshufflings of desire like a single held note under a succession of lesser ones; they have occupied the seats separating Mark from Ellen like twin resistors in a closed circuit. Sunlight passes through the fluted iced-tea pitcher to Ellen's left, casting a warm brown shadow on her hand. Watching Mark wait for her answer, Ellen decides "No" again.

"Okay," she says. "Can you pass the rice pilaf, please?"

The truth is, Ellen Borneo has been at Slow Hill Colony three weeks, and she still hasn't gotten anything done. She's fallen into a routine and, unfortunately, work doesn't seem to play much of a part in it.

Part of the problem, undoubtedly, is the hours. The kitchen bell rings at seven-thirty. Breakfast is served from eight until nine. If Ellen goes, she eats, drinks, waves away cigarette smoke, and is in her cabin by (at the earliest) ten. If she skips breakfast, she gets to her cabin by nine, and is hungry by eleven.

The next problem is her cabin. Everyone at Slow Hill gets his own cabin—the place, Ellen thinks, is a sort of Walden Pond Motor Court or Henry Thoreau Bungalow Lodge. All the cabins have fireplaces, and Ellen loves fires. Her first morning she lit one, without first remembering to open the flue. Black smoke poured into the room, dribbling up over the mantelpiece, setting off the smoke alarm, striping and stippling in the window's morning sun. With a *whoosh*, Ellen put it out with the fire extinguisher (secretly, she'd always wanted to use one). The next morning, arriving promptly at nine fortified by coffee and a contact nicotine high, Ellen found her cabin stinking so strongly of smoke and sulfur that she couldn't enter. She walked to the office and picked up five cans of room deodorizer, used them till each began to emptily rattle and ping. Now, Ellen's cabin has three distracting odors: smoke, sulfur, and pine. The component aromas, she thinks, of an extinguished forest fire.

Lunch is the next problem. It is delivered to each cabin at noon by a bearded, ponytailed man driving the colony's rattling green truck. If Ellen is working, this truck breaks her concentration. If she's not, the *idea* of the truck does: why start working if you're just going to be interrupted in an hour or so anyway? Ellen's solution, so far, has been not to work at all, at least in the mornings.

And then after lunch—peanut-butter-and-cream-cheese sandwiches, Mint Milanos in a translucent wax paper sheath, a heavy cool Thermos of blood-thick V-8 juice—it doesn't seem wise to work, either. Eating makes Ellen sleepy. There's no reason to start work unless you're fresh, and can bring to it your best self. So Ellen naps, from one until three. When she awakes words, in her stuffy head, seem as thick and coagulated as her V-8 juice. Ellen spends her afternoons outdoors, reading in one of the damp-smelling Adirondack chairs by Colony Hall. But by the time she has brought herself back around to the power of words, insects are springing up from the cooling grass at her ankles, the sun is already beginning its inexorable nosedive to the west. The dinner bell will ring at five-thirty. Why work, etc.?

And then after dinner—during which she promises herself she'll return to her cabin—Ellen simply lacks the energy. She's been worrying about work all day: now she's too exhausted to do any. Plus, as Ellen sees it, you're only allowed so much self per any given day. If you squeeze it out in conversation (as Ellen must, to be polite at dinner), you can't have enough left over for fiction. Ellen's smoky cabin at the edge of the woods is far less appealing than another beer, or more ice cream, or a movie on the colony VCR. Watching these movies—*Friday the 13th,* all lights out, the way Ellen likes watching television least—Ellen can't help hating herself. Her fellow colonists applaud the dumber dialogue, laugh at the spectacular killings, showily and collectively lowering their standards after a hard day of privately employing them in their cabins. In bed, back in her room, planning out what she'll do the next morning, Ellen feels an unpleasant pressure welling up against the backs of her eyes. Mosquitoes whine over her head, and seem to land by her ear. She swats at them. There's nothing there. The jerky shapes bounce in the moonlight, as if being flown by supporting wires. Ellen finds tears on her cheeks. Mosquitoes descend towards the puddles. She has less than two weeks to go, and Ellen Borneo is going crazy at Slow Hill.

Ellen had been living in New York for two years when her agent sent her to Slow Hill. Nothing was going well. Ellen couldn't start anything, and what she started couldn't finish.

It's too bad, because Ellen knows if she could just squeeze something out (at Slow Hill or back in the city), she would be successful. Her college friends work in publishing, at newspapers and magazines. They have pledged themselves to review her work favorably. Her agent knows editors, publicity people, the buyers for bookstore chains. A huge network of people is waiting to help rumble her forward. But in the face of all these primed mechanisms Ellen's fiction pales, becomes a tiny, fragile thing, like a frightened monkey strapped in behind the controls of a rocket.

Ellen published her first stories in college and graduate school. Her agent (he was not her agent then), reading the third—about the vegetarian boyfriend her heroine abandons and then sheepishly returns to one winter in Bermuda—called and invited her to lunch. Ellen took a deep breath, and went. She ordered salad. When it arrived, she knew it to be a terrible mistake. Shredded red lettuce and broccoli fronds kept catching at the sides of her mouth, making her look, she felt, like some absurd marshy dinosaur. The agent pretended not to notice. His own filet mignon he ate with marvelous efficiency, cutting it into strips in advance, so that he could then deposit the pieces in his mouth without having to break conversation. Ellen imagined the neat sections, in his stomach, re-forming themselves into a perfect steak. He made his pitch, in which he pretended to convince Ellen to join him and Ellen pretended to weigh her options, but even he didn't seem that interested. His eyes, having already extracted what was necessary from Ellen's, dulled, and then roved, to other diners and then to the waiter. The waiter returned. The agent made a little show of paying, with his firm's American Express card, but Ellen could see that the bill was in fact not that high. She could have paid it herself, with the rumpled cash in her front jeans pocket. The agent caught her eyes reading, and so tried to make the gesture with a small flourish of magnanimity, but Ellen had the distressing sense, in that instant, that there was a grandeur you expected for the important moments in life, to which actual events couldn't quite manage to rise.

After this complex welcome to the publishing world, Ellen didn't write anything publishable for a year. She taught two sections of beginning fiction and struggled. In May, her agent called with two queries, the first being, Would Ellen like to go to Slow Hill? Ellen said yes, though she thought it was difficult to get in, you had to apply, get recommendations. In reply, her agent rattled off the names of three famous authors, all clients, all of whom would be willing, though they'd never read a word of Ellen's fiction, to recommend her. Her agent's tone, since Ellen had failed, over a year's worth of nights, to become an overnight success, had grown exasperated, like a teacher keeping a student very long after school. "Second question," he said. "How'd you like to meet Dale Kohler?"

At Slow Hill, all the other colonists talk about is "work." Ellen arrived with high hopes, stepping out of the taxi, her shirt soaked and wrinkled from six hours on the Greyhound. The colony looked beautiful, small birds everywhere, making little arching dips between trees like the telephone wires she'd seen from the window of the bus. As she walked into Colony Hall to read the names on the mailboxes, Ellen assumed the other colonists would be a famous bunch, all successes like her recommenders, and that in joining them she was taking a step towards becoming success-ful herself.

But the other colonists in their real lives were assistant professors, travel-journalists, word processors. They were older than Ellen and mostly in the same boat, only, by virtue of their having been in the water longer, a little farther along in the current. They talked about work all day. In the mornings, between cigarettes, they talked about how much work they were going to do. In the evenings, at dinner, they discussed how much work they'd done. Had there been telephones in the cabins, they probably would have talked at lunch, about how much work they were doing. Ellen hates talking about work—it's too easy to confuse the pleasure in talking about something with the pleasure in doing it. But the other colonists talk about work with a kind of despera-tion. It's as if they study French all year, and the colony is

Paris. This is a language they get to speak only on special occasions.

Mark at first impressed Ellen by not talking about work at all. She had been at Slow Hill two weeks, and when Mark sat down in the empty seat across from her (the hawk-faced woman, writing about her rabbi's Yom Kippur, was for accuracy skipping dinner; in her place was a pale poet doing a series on the joys of celibacy, he and the priest were comparing notes) there seemed to be an immediate understanding between them. It was the same as, when a child, Ellen had gone visiting with her parents. There was always, as a bribe for her, a child her own age there, and there would be, beneath the heated, resentful embarrassment of falling into preassigned roles, the understanding between whatever strange girl and Ellen that they would soon become friends. After dinner, Ellen and Mark walked to the corner of Colony Hall—a huge, pleasant room, colonists' bedrooms upstairs. They were drinking beer, and were already a little drunk. Some colonists were playing Ping-Pong, and others pool, and still others were watching the basketball play-offs on TV, and so to the sound of clicking, rolling, and bouncing balls, Ellen and Mark talked. Cheers kept coming from the TV room, making Ellen feel curiously exposed, and adored.

Mark was from New Orleans. He lived in New York now, in the East 20s. He intimated he was writing about Louisiana, and when Ellen asked, "Why didn't you keep living there?" Mark lit a cigarette, tipped his head back a little, and joked, "Well, if Joyce had to leave Ireland to write about Dublin," letting the rest of the sentence hang with his gray, cloudy exhalation over their heads. A cheer rose from the other room, and this remark, which would have been inexcusable in any other environment, seemed okay here, since it was so clearly (Ellen hoped) a joke. There was still, since he had just

arrived, the scent of New York about Mark, an aloofness
which after two weeks in New Hampshire Ellen felt had
been puffed out of her. It quickened her blood to imagine the
same clothes he was wearing now being put on in a dark
apartment near Gramercy Park, to imagine them on a
subway, in Port Authority, making their way here. And she
liked how, though Mark was heavy, he wore his dark shirt
tucked in, not trying to use its untucked length to hide his
thighs. He was heavy. So? With his black jeans and sneakers,
he had a clear sense of style, and Ellen found that attractive.
If men had clear senses of style, of what clothes looked good
on them, it usually meant they had stable senses of self. Too
often, Ellen had found, in the worst cases, men tried to use
women to provide one for them.

For some minutes, Ellen had been aware she was shred-
ding the gold-foil neck of her beer bottle with her thumbnail.
Now, a whole section peeled away in her hand. She held it
out to Mark, to show him, and he took it from her and
tucked it back into the pocket of her shirt. For a moment, the
back of his hand brushed her breast. Ellen felt a surge, and
decided, conversely, not to sleep with him. For the five
weeks she was at Slow Hill, Ellen was trying to keep her
brain uncluttered.

In the spring before she met him, two books Dale Kohler
had edited had become literary best-sellers. When he stepped
into the office where Ellen was already waiting—his window
overlooked Union Square Park, which had recently been
remodeled to discourage muggings—he seemed unaccus-
tomed to his new success, and moved about in it gingerly, as
in a new suit he wasn't completely sure he wouldn't return.
He sat down behind his desk, Ellen sat in front of it. She
concentrated on the books on his shelf, to keep from

becoming too nervous. Kohler asked questions, about where she'd gone to school, what she was doing now. Ellen answered. After fifteen minutes, it became clear that he had as little idea as to why the meeting was taking place as she did. Ellen's agent had made the appointment, after all; Kohler hadn't asked for it. In another situation, this might have made Ellen more comfortable, put them both on the same, hazy side. Now, it made her speak more rapidly. She talked about her fiction—brushing her hair back and straightening her pink-framed glasses, which she'd worn expressly for this meeting—but she experienced one of those hideous moments race car drivers and airline pilots must experience, as their steering fails and their machines begin to spin out of control. The connection between her brain and mouth—and through it the world—had slipped. She wanted to come off witty and fun, but what she was sounding, she realized from a worried nick in Kohler's expression, was incomprehensible.

When she was finished, Kohler nodded many times— Ellen wasn't even sure what she'd just said—and picked up a pencil. "Those pieces you published were really striking. Do you have anything else in the works?"

"Oh," Ellen said, and once again some important mechanism failed her, "I haven't really tried yet. I just thought I'd finish a few things before I began polishing them up and sending them around, which always makes me nervous, sending things out one at a time, because then I just sit around waiting for the mail to come in and don't do anything at all."

Kohler blinked very rapidly, taking this in. He fiddled around on his desk for a moment and then, with an air of decision, handed Ellen a thick, salmon-colored paperback with the publishing house's insignia on the cover. "Here," he said. "This is our summer catalog. I thought you might like to have it." And then he relaxed; he'd gotten the matter sorted out. Ellen had come down to personally pick up a copy of the catalog.

Which, to calm herself down, Ellen looked through, for books by authors her own age. "What are you doing this summer?" Kohler asked, and for a moment the connection between her brain and ears seemed to have slipped too, for Kohler had italicized the "you."

"Oh," Ellen said, "I'm going to Slow Hill for a few weeks in June.'"

Kohler brightened further. He'd found a terminal point for their conversation. He laced his fingers behind his neck, forming a little T-shaped pillow which his head overlapped like the arrow in a crossbow. "Great," he said. "That should be very productive for you. Show me your stuff when you get back."

At Slow Hill, Ellen tries anything to get out of her rut. She jogs in the afternoons. It's dragonfly season in New Hampshire, and as she runs she finds tiny, bottle-green corpses curled and dying all over the road. Like deer, she supposes, they have been hit by cars, though the drivers have not noticed. They move their long tails and try to flip themselves over onto their bellies, to give their wings a better chance. When Ellen can fit it into the rhythm of her stride, she crushes them underfoot, putting them out of their misery. But back in her cabin, sweaty, head buzzing and brain jostled, she can't begin to work. She passes Mark one afternoon, and he calls out, "Ellen! How's the work coming?"

Another night she tries sleeping in her cabin. At home, she always sleeps in the same room she works in, and maybe this is what's been missing. After dinner, she forgoes Mark's invitation to *A Nightmare on Elm Street* and his mock-sad "We'll miss you" to return to the woods. The evening is not a success. There are too many noises, the cabin itself is cold. Ellen can't sleep. At eleven, she switches on the light, and this activates the June bugs outside her window. They keep banging against the panes, wobbling a few feet backwards to get up steam, then slamming into the panes again. Ellen goes to her window to watch them, these round, furry creatures retreating and advancing like frenzied pendulums, and finds it's not just the June bugs—multitudes of insects are slithering over the outside of her window, trying to get in. A moth skitters along the mullions, flapping its gray wings so quickly it seems a flickering image from a silent movie. Another insect, with a kind of funnel mouth, sucks desperately at the glass, tiny lungs pulsing, tiny heart beating. Ellen tries rapping the window, but this doesn't discourage the insects. Her room contains a miniature sun, and they want to be back in daylight. She thinks of herself, pressing against Kohler's desk in his office. Shots from *Friday the 13th* recur to her, grisly murders the colonists applauded days ago. Ellen pictures herself in every scene, stalked by axes, menaced by machetes, hooded lunatics bursting into her cabin. She shuts the lights, grabs her flashlight, and runs to Colony Hall, which, with its yellow lights blazing from every window, seems a kind of brave outpost against the night. Mark is in the TV room with the younger colonists, watching the climax of the movie. A young girl is being pursued through a house by a hooded maniac. "Miss me?" Mark asks, mock-hopeful.

In a way, Ellen thinks, the whole idea of a colony is a mistake. Why would someone think that bringing you to a new place, with nothing there to remind you who you are, would help you express yourself better? Ellen dislikes everything about Slow Hill. She particularly dislikes the way the other colonists get along, their good fellowship. Don't they realize they're competing for an infinitesimal number of spots in the real world? Graduate school had annoyed her in just this way, all the students friendly, encouraging each other, when what they should have been doing was erasing each other's disks, mis-editing stories, damaging grammar. Every person who became published occupied a space they couldn't.

Here at Slow Hill, as there, everyone is supportive. At readings in the library—which are uniformly bad—everything is praised. Each story is "the best of that type I've ever heard," or, at least, full of "nice imagery." It's as though with every compliment the colonists think they're buying themselves one in return. In graduate school, everyone (Ellen too) had engaged in just this sort of lobbying; when a story of yours was up, you got extra nice to people before class. But Ellen had assumed this would end with graduate school. What do the colonists think? That when people buy a book of theirs, or when editors or reviewers receive it in the mail, they can follow those people home, compliment their drapes, their kids, their dogs, and *then* have them read their work?

After one reading, during the flashlit walk back from Colony Library to Colony Hall, Mark catches up with Ellen. "What'd you think?" he asks. His body next to hers is a dark silhouette.

"It was awful," Ellen says. "I can't believe you liked it."

"Oh, well, come on," Mark says, in a confiding tone, "you have to say something." She hears a scratch and then a hissing flare, and a moment later Mark is a dark silhouette with a glowing red tip at its upper edge. He makes an exhaling sound. There is a familiar, mixed smell of sulfur and smoke, which makes Ellen think guiltily of her cabin. She shines her flashlight straight up, at the stars. Insects appear in the cone of light.

"I hope you're easier on me," Mark is going on, "when I read Thursday."

And Ellen whirls on him, shining her flashlight on his face. He's lobbying! Mark shields his eyes with a complaining expression; his nostrils cast arching shadows over his cheeks, his skin is very white. "This is like my writing class," she says, directing the light back at the gravel.

Mark seems to know what she means. "Confidentially," he says, "I don't have anything near ready. I'm just going to spend the afternoon putting together the worst shit I can think of, to see what they'll say."

Will, Ellen's ex-boyfriend, had been a vegetarian. It had been one of the first things about him to annoy her, for it had seemed a futile attempt at control, to control even his insides, forever asking waitresses, "Is your corn chowder made with vegetable stock?" Ellen had been with him three years, one year longer than she'd wanted. At first, the confusion of being back in New York, after graduate school, had kept her with him—watching as her friends bought furniture at Conran's and Workbench, clever furniture which, in a pinch, could always double as something else, a couch that became a futon-bed, a table that was also a desk. Then there was the shock of watching as quirks which, in college, had seemed charming now were revealed as dangerous and ugly flaws. One girl, for example, who had been so brilliant in school that she could never keep her papers on the assigned topic, and never could decide on a major, became, with her inability to choose a career or even to produce a résumé, a flake, an example of what to avoid.

Later, as Ellen struggled, she began to blame Will. Something in her environment was holding her back, and—though they lived in separate apartments—her environment was Will. She kept being afraid he would turn her into a vegetarian; whenever she ate meat, he would stare at her with a sad, forgiving expression, as if he were the dead animal's mother. And she, who, as a spectator, had always enjoyed watching the strategies with which men courted her, resented that Will no longer seemed to feel it necessary to court at all. He sprawled in her apartment, confident of being adored. It was May, and Ellen felt her life moving towards a kind of delta: if she came back from Slow Hill with good pieces, she could go to Dale Kohler; if not, she would have to find more teaching. But how exactly, if she couldn't get her fiction published, was she qualified to teach? What she resented most about Will was that he made her feel comfortable. Even their love-making had become an aspect of comforting, a question he asked with his body, to which hers affirmatively responded. They had become, she thought, less like lovers than like siblings, a brother and sister who had once, with some fanfare and excitement, crossed the incest barrier, and now did so only out of dull habit, now that they were grown and there was little chance of their parents discovering and bursting in. The world couldn't accept being seen by someone comfortable, was what Ellen feared, and yet relationships did that, dulled things, like the translucent second eyelid an alligator lowers over its eyes before swimming underwater. Ellen left Will before coming here.

Thursday night, in the library, Mark reads his story to the colonists. It's terrible. The plot keeps reminding Ellen of something she's read, or seen, somewhere. She can't remember, quite, but she knows the plot twists as they come up.

There is no dialogue. A man walks across a ruined landscape, in a sort of uniform ("his epaulet brushed his unshaven cheek"). He comes to a town devastated by cataclysm, the bent spokes of an abandoned bicycle giving off "the empty glow of fallout." There is a woman in the wreckage, also in uniform. She is American; he is Russian. They look at each other with great understanding, the two last soldiers, last people, on Earth. Each pulls a gun. As Mark, his voice earnest and slow, reads the climax, in which the man and woman put aside their differences for the greater good of replenishing the race, Ellen remembers: it's an old *Twilight Zone* episode. She lowers her head. The colonists sit in silence, breathing slowly, letting the last few lines sink in.

"Really strong," someone says.

"It makes you think about war," a woman says.

"You know what you should do? Send it to *Mother Jones*. They're doing fiction now. It's perfect for them. It's about *glasnost*."

Then there is the rumble of movement, as the one group, following social formulae of its own, metastasizes into several smaller ones, everyone going for the potato chips and beer that are served at the readings. One group moves around Mark, to congratulate him. He grins at Ellen. Ellen grins back, though she thinks, in a way, that it would have been nice to hear his own stuff, which she imagines as humid and sticky, New Orleans couples separating in stifling apartments overlooking tired palms.

"You do all that up here?" someone asks Mark.

"Most," Mark replies, with his slight accent. "I've had the main idea for a while."

"Ellen," a heavy voice booms behind her. It's one of the recent arrivals, a large composer whose name Ellen hasn't learned but who has chosen to ingratiate himself with the community by confiding in as many people—and by getting as many people to confide in him—as possible. His own work, he has already revealed at dinner, is a comic opera based on the Alger Hiss trial. He flips a potato chip into his mouth and claps down hard on it, a single, spine-smashing crunch, as if for emphasis. Ellen winces, sympathetically. "When are you going to favor us with your own work? We're beginning to wonder what you *do* all day, in that cabin of yours."

Her last two days, Ellen's agent calls. Ellen knows why he is calling, and doesn't call back. Will calls. Ellen is sitting at the table when he does, and can tell, from a certain quality in the ringing pay phone (and from a corresponding drop in her stomach) that it is him. She tells Mark to say she isn't there. He looks at her quizzically, and goes back to the phone.

In her cabin the last days, Ellen can't think of a story she could finish in a week, and so never starts one. The problem is that any decision invalidates all others, and under the weight of all the rejected options no one decision ever seems right. So Ellen sits in the Adirondack chair all day, from morning to evening, through all the hot hours sandwiched in between. Her agent calls again. Ellen answers in a fake voice. Her agent says, "Tell Ellen I'm waiting."

Her last night at Slow Hill there is a small party. She, the priest, and the hawk-faced woman are all leaving in the morning. Paper placemats are passed around—a Slow Hill tradition—to each person in the dining room, to pen their names, phone numbers, addresses. Perhaps the priest and the hawk-faced woman will keep in contact—their protagonists can sleep together—but Ellen can't imagine seeing any of these people in New York, in her real life. Her placemat returns to her, grease-marked. The other colonists are already back to talking and laughing, subtly shunning Ellen and the other two at her table now that the secret is out, everyone knows they won't be here tomorrow. Death. This is what death will be like, Ellen thinks. There will be a moment's pause, as everyone considers you, and then a general return to happiness, flirting, merriment. Things will go on, spinning away.

After dinner, final readings are given, by the priest and the hawk-faced woman. In her novel, the lady rabbi is giving a sermon when a penis inscribed with the tetragrammaton comes lolling out of the Torah. In a surprise switch, she becomes a Catholic layperson. Ellen looks at the priest, sitting in a worn plum easy chair, listening, with a tensed smile, both to the hawk-faced woman's words and, on a subtler frequency, for the colonist's reactions to them. Of course, these two have been lovers all along; how could Ellen not have seen it until now? The priest stands and reads a brief poem, "Coital Catechism," which is arranged question-and-answer style.

After this, because it is still light—the second-longest day of the year—there is volleyball, outside, gnats hovering around them in blurry revolving cones, the ball spanking and pinkening Ellen's forearms, the low sun giving every-thing a funny gray light that makes Ellen's stomach jumpy. Mark is on her team. "Work, Ellen, work!" he calls, when she is making a difficult shot. Ellen ignores him. Just as she is dead to the colony, so he, with his touching, still-ready look, is dead to her. There is beer afterwards. Ellen feels curious inside, the jumpy feeling spreading from her stom-ach along her spine and then all the way up to her head. The colonists are back inside Colony Hall, drinking and delightedly eating the evening's special snack, buttered sweet corn. How funny to call this a colony! When so obviously it's not the colony but the motherland, life's too easy here to be a colony. It's the colony Ellen feels she's returning to, a teeming, unlawful port, New York is like that sometimes, a Portuguese inroad in East Africa. The people here, sipping iced tea and beer with their legs crossed, watching the sun finally set and the lightning bugs alternately immolate and extinguish themselves, are not colonists at all. But Ellen is. She has been colonizing all her life. College was like colonizing, until it became, by a kind of warp, home, and then graduate school was colonizing, and then just living in New York, moving to New York, was like the journey to some primitive village, where living space was scarce and even plumbing somehow communal, for whenever anyone used her apartment's bathroom Ellen had to politely pretend she couldn't hear them pee. Love has been colonizing, too. Will tried to colonize her, but he had failed, she'd expelled him, and yet in a way she still longed for him, because he had changed her. It is through these thoughts, and not the darkened main hall—the sounds of Ping-Pong starting up again, the TV newscaster blandly reading the bland, Nashua, New Hampshire, news—that Ellen drifts. She will be returning to her difficult city tomorrow, on the Greyhound, as if on an overcrowded boat and for the first time.

She is unsurprised to see Mark waiting in the corner of the hall, corn cob in his soft plastic beer glass, grinning sheepishly. Without saying anything, she takes his hand and walks him upstairs, to her room, one step ahead as though on a trail. Mark asks, "How's the work coming?" and inside her room they are kissing, Ellen tasting the mingled tastes of cigarettes and corn in his mouth, and behind that, beneath them both, like the continuo in a piece of music, the dark taste of beer. There are glints of unfamiliar teeth, and a roughness different from Will's; Mark hasn't shaved, quite, the area around his lips.

And though Ellen skips ahead, lying in bed with him, and sees the dreary days to come—Gramercy Park under snow, waiting for Mark to call, or being afraid he will call—now as she and Mark move together, Ellen feels tethers being released, she is floating, and paragraphs are blooming, phrases are unsnapping and unfolding themselves, words are assembling themselves behind her eyes.

WORLD OF AIRPLANES

I F HE DID NOT MARRY HER, he had begun to think, he was a cad. Worse was the thought that if he did marry her, he was still a cad. But in their last fight—he trying vainly to convince her that he was willing to hang around, but it would *only* be hanging around, he was blocking the outward path of her life like a boulder—when he suggested she try to meet another man, she said, "I'm too old." When he countered her on this, asked, "What do you mean?" (for the pattern of their fights was to extract self-incriminating outbursts from her, which they would then, like two disinterested specialists, examine for underlying content), she shook her head, made believe she hadn't said it at all, and changed the subject completely, to *his* failings.

Only what she couldn't realize—staring snuffy-faced at him across a table at the Mad Hatter, over inlaid menus which, with the helplessness of ex–English majors, neither of them could resist reading during lulls in the conversation—was that what he was doing was done out of love, in a way. He did not want to imagine her life locked with his, in an embrace in which she would forever love him and he not her. On the phone the next morning, they went over the same material again, comparing their results. Jenny thought they'd decided to make a go of it; Steven's results were somewhat different. They argued and argued, as if there were indeed a set of facts which could be impersonally inspected, objectively tallied, and Steven did not have the heart to burst in that the fact was that *he did not love her.* He did not love her.

He had lived in her house all fall, and felt he understood her better, now, than at any time during their four years. But it was the understanding we have for ourselves, which exists without emotion, only with a certain exhaustion at our own patterns. He had found in her desk an index card saying, "The last time I will be ten," followed, a few lines later, in a more pointedly adult script, by, "The first time I will be eleven." She'd signed both statements. It was sweet, but not the basis, exactly, for an erotic relationship. The house was a white, two-story clapboard in Southport, Connecticut. Living there, among the polished surfaces, the garbage disposal (which he broke the first week; there was a protesting grinding and then a quick, blink-fast snap; the mangled, misplaced spoons emerged as if from a fight with some monstrous serpent), Steven had felt locked inside Jenny's brain, inside her skull. His own personality, with no one to exercise it upon, had ceased to matter. He looked through windows that were her windows, ate off dishes that were her dishes, heard—during the surprisingly cool October nights—ticks from the heating system that was her heating system. He had never felt so swallowed, so engulfed, before.

Steven had moved to Jenny's parent's house to finish studying for his law boards. Steven had known Jenny was rich for as long as he'd known Jenny—it was one of the things that had announced itself to him when he met her at school, in her silk windbreaker and black, October gloves:

I'm rich. It had been an attraction, but not as evil a one as it would come to seem later. He had thought to himself, as he kissed her the first time, in the front seat of her car, Now I'm going to see what rich girls are like. It was the same dispassionate, fairly anxious voice with which he'd announced to himself, the first day of ninth grade, So this is high school, and, as he walked through his apartment after his first day of real work, This is what adult life is. That day—eighteen months ago—he had walked with a cigarette and a Lite beer to his futon and flipped on the news: All the pleasures adult life had kept in store for him, the little trust fund of behavior the culture had waited to bestow until his twenty-first year. Now it was his.

But he had never presumed, with Jenny, to use her wealth before. It had been a room, in the structure of her personality, into which he never ventured; its contents were too delicate, too liable, it seemed, to be shattered by the first clumsy exploration. His first year in New York had been disappointing, the publishing work he'd taken on (serving as a kind of secretary to a sour-faced junior editor) less interesting than he'd hoped. School had been juicier—people all around, with their aggressive styles and assertive modes of speech, all that promise laid up ahead of them, all that jaunty energy so that when he saw the many Géricault studies for the *Running of the Barbary Horses* this had crystallized into his feelings for college. His publishing colleagues were all dealing, in their various ways, with diminished expectations. Shelly, the girl his own age there, hired that fall with him, looked sourer each day, as each day brought with it another disappointment: Her apartment fell through, she was forced to move from Brooklyn Heights to Hoboken, the alternate job she applied for, as a fact checker with a fashion magazine—itself a comedown from the magazines where she would have liked to work—failed to materialize. Her skin grew paler in the winter, her haircuts more eccentric and her clothes—the collection of folded-back men's jackets and odd, policeman-style shoes—more determinedly, aggressively unsuitable, as if daring the world to make final this last disappointment. "I'm ready to go home, Steven," she told him, at lunch in the building's sadly lit cafeteria. "I mean it; four months ago, nothing seemed worse than imagining myself running into my mother's bedroom and crying into her lap. Now I can't imagine anything more attractive. I'll finally have a place to do my laundry." Steven had become, on his own, continually optimistic, to deflect her pessimism; their conversations had seemed to demand the accommodations of yin and yang.

Yet when she was fired, finally, in April—she had stopped coming to work entirely, in pursuit of other jobs—it was Steven who was disappointed and sad. The actual position of his life struck him: It was as if the lenses he'd worn to console this girl had consoled him too. With their removal he saw his office, his tiny apartment, clearly, in their natural light. He began to sink: He felt as if a certain amount of spirit, juiciness, had been removed from him too, and he reminded himself, sadly, that Géricault hadn't found it in him to finish the *Barbary Horses* picture. It had remained a series of varying sketches. The painter had been dispirited by all that spirit.

Through all this dispiritedness Jenny had flitted. She traveled in and out of New York, lived in a glorious apartment on the Upper West Side, in a building overlooking the back of the Museum of Natural History. Jenny's father— her parents were divorced—owned companies in France and Palo Alto, and Jenny had cheerfully taken on the role of his aide in management, a puckish spirit, or, when Steven thought about it, more Grecian, Iris raining down with

Zeus's commands onto the disobedient fields of Ilium. When the board of a software company wanted to launch their product behind the agreed-upon design schedule, and Mr. Fuld could not attend their meeting, Jenny went as his emissary and, with threatened thunderbolts, brought them back into submission. Staying in her apartment when she was not there, weekends and sometimes whole weeks, had been Steven's first giving in in the face of what he now realized had been a commandment to himself: that he never use her things, or allow them to influence his decision to stay with her. In the spring, when he looked at Jenny, what he saw was not the girl he'd first kissed Junior year, on the way back from a soccer game, her lips dry with the first week of steam heat in her house and her tongue surprisingly cold, like a cherry bomb pop. What he saw was her apartment, with its large kitchen and CD player and sleek VCR and fine park view. The yin to his own yang of disappointment.

In June, Shelly turned up at his office, looking once more lively and jaunty. Her last note to him, on their company's stationery, had been, "April: The cruelest month." There was nothing cruel-looking about her now. She sauntered over to his desk—he did not have an office, just a battered old Wang console under a bookshelf, out of the way of a corridor—in the defiant shorts and T-shirt of the non-worker. The color had returned to her face, her hair was more accommodating to the shape of her skull. She took Steven to lunch, where he waited for her to confess what she did indeed confess: she was returning to school, her parents had been happy to pay, she'd met a man. She was living at home for the summer, in Bethesda. "You look worse for wear, Steven," she said, after a pointed pause, as if by absenting herself from the world of work she had absented herself from the world of social convention as well.

"Jesus, I feel it," Steven said, and their positions were

reversed, suddenly, Shelly telling him how much she admired his sticking it out in the city, at their old job, and Steven finally saying to someone (the bubble of confession had expanded in his throat many times, talking to Jenny, but had never before quite burst) how unhappy he was, how he hated his job, and how his life seemed, "I don't know, cloudy somehow. It felt sunny before, years ago. Honestly, I never knew what people meant, when they said they were depressed. I'd be unhappy, about a bad grade or something, but not for weeks on end. Now, I wake up, and my head always feels tingly around the back of the neck, and I keep wondering why I'm doing what I'm doing."

Shelly adroitly changed the subject. She asked about Jenny, whom they had spoken about, in the flirting way an available woman will talk about a girlfriend with a man. "God, I can't stand her sometimes," he said, feeling more bubbles swelling. "She just travels in and out of the country all the time, she had to get a new passport, honestly, she'd run out of space on the old one." And though Steven knew, on some level, that he hadn't been feeling spite all year, when he spoke these words they became, by a kind of twisted alchemy, his feelings. Memories, he thought, were like clay, awaiting a final twist; when we characterize them, we breathe in souls. Now the whole, creaky year stood up and shambled before Steven, animated by this pronouncement. He hated Jenny because she skittered above him, above depression. A part of his life gasped at the untruth of this, but it was pushed away, silenced forever. Shelly watched, glittering-eyed. She had a new man, a boy from her old college, but she could not help enjoying this final evisceration of Steven and Jenny. Some of her old competitive spirit had been roused, the same way, Steven thought, that Jenny would sometimes curse when reading in the paper of the defeat of her prep school by some other. These passions, which he had thought theatrical, were real, and could be reanimated with the barest flicker.

By the summer, a new callousness had entered their relationship. Steven had glimpsed a truth: He was using Jenny. It was a sad truth, but like most such it was one he could use. Reminding himself of it reminded him that he was cruel, and these reminders helped. He had been Jenny's first lover. Her sophistication had been a gauze hiding this fact. Her life had consisted of so many connecting flights—to boarding school, to Gstaadt for skiing, to her divorced parents' houses for different holidays—that she had never had a long enough layover to take a lover. Steven saw, lying with her on her father's Zodiac boat in the Connecticut sound, that he could use this against her. That she would, in all likelihood, never leave him first. She had no basis for judging the appropriateness or inappropriateness of his actions. She was like the water all around them: she reflected things, had not yet acquired the opacity of experience.

That she loved him was clear enough to Steven. They stayed the whole week of his vacation in her father's house on Canfield Island, in Connecticut. They borrowed his Acura and made forays into Southport, to her mother's new home and to the old one, which had reverted to the children after the divorce. Neither parent had wanted it—it had been the gooey middle of the eggshell halves to which both had retreated. "Who lives here?" Steven asked, in his J. Crew T-shirt and shorts, in the kitchen of this house, where one overhead fluorescent refused to light but also refused to extinguish, and kept pulsing on and off with an unnatural, arrhythmic intensity.

"No one anymore. You could live here," Jenny said, chewing her poppy-seed bagel. "Dump that apartment of yours and come see what the country is like. I've been trying to get you out here for years."

This was true: he had resisted discovering just how wealthy Jenny was, for fear this would cloud his judgment of her. Parents on both sides had been tacitly off-limits. What he couldn't judge now was how seriously Jenny had intended the offer. After making it, she turned one of the feathery pages of the *Times* magazine, which argued, depressingly, that the gesture had been off-hand. Or maybe she had sensed Steven's intensity, and was trying to fend him off.

Back in New York, however, at the end of August, with his tan absorbed by his office-mates and the city sweltering, the image of the house, empty in these autumn months, haunted Steven. He pictured himself living in Jenny's bedroom, jogging around the tiny town, driving to the supermarket. Only the question of what he was doing there eluded him. He lived, as he went about his business of typing the junior editor's letters to a more senior one, a phantom life in Southport. He was in sweatpants, trotting up and down the stairs, floppy, insouciant again, champing at the bit. But what was he doing there?

He was studying. It came to him slowly. The costume of his fantasy he'd borrowed from his last year of college; thus he was studying for something. But what? It was a friend of Jenny's, over sushi at a restaurant, who provided this answer. They were rubbing the backs of their balsa-wood chopsticks together, a ritual Steven had learned to copy at college—they seemed to be trying to make fire, which struck him as pleasingly primitive in advance of these overly refined meals of pastel-colored, soy-sauced fish—and which he'd only recently made sense of. It removed the possibility of splinters. Jenny's friend was talking about her Stanley

Kaplan course, her Princeton Review course. She was taking the law boards October First.

"I'd like to take those too, I think," Steven said.

Both girls turned to him together. "It's too late for Kaplan," Jenny's friend said.

And Jenny said, "You'd better just study. It's only a month, and they're excruciating."

And Steven had his plan, his opening. He ate the meal hurriedly, shoveling the gingery salad, breaking up the doughy mustard into his soy sauce, chewing down the pasty bits of rice and fish. After they'd seen the other girl home, ejected her from their cab into her apartment, Steven turned to Jenny (drunk on Sapporo; she liked to think she didn't drink, and at dinner would suggest that Steven order beer after beer, which they would then split) and mentioned that he needed a place to go, where he could simply study, without the pressures of rent and work and socializing. A place for just a few weeks, secluded—

"Why not my house—my mom's house, I mean. You know, Southport?"

Steven at first poo-pooed the idea, careful not to spoil things by seeming over-eager. But he did appear to weigh the pros and cons. "Would your parents mind?" he asked.

"I don't see why," Jenny said, and Steven was suddenly intimidated by, of all people, the cabbie, who had looked up in the mirror and leaned his head back, as if to listen in on their conversation. The driver was Steven's cohort in poverty, and would see, beneath the delicate skimming Steven was trying to achieve, the ugly manipulations at bottom. With his eyes, squinting them, Steven urged Jenny to discretion. "I don't see why," Jenny repeated, in a raspy whisper. "No one's staying there. I'm sure my mom would be happy to have someone taking care of the place."

As if to make clear his independence, Steven did not sleep

at Jenny's, but on the futon in his studio, which had become increasingly flat and lumpy, like a sheet laid out over wet towels. The next morning, when he called Jenny at work, he waited for some invitation in her voice to bring the subject up again. Had it been a drunken pleasantry? Jenny had the slightly polished sound she got at her office, as though her voice were wearing glossy makeup. No invitation came, and finally Steven chanced, "Jenny, I was thinking about what we said last night."

"Fabulous," Jenny said, as if she'd been waiting all along for Steven to broach the subject. "Super. Go up whenever you want. I think it's a great idea."

And after various phone calls, and after Steven's shopping the bookstores for their LSAT guides, and after a dash through cavernous Grand Central Station, Steven found himself living in Connecticut. Jenny's motives were less clear than his, but she seemed happy to have him in her home, vaguely triumphant. He had ventured into a room which, out of silly squeamishness, he had been avoiding for years. Now she had him inside it. He sensed a dangerousness, almost, in her manner, as she showed him the house, its various functions, this old white fort in which his spirit was expected to thrive.

But it did not thrive, exactly, though he studied all morning, perfecting the various problems, learning to make charts for the "logic" questions. Jenny called every other night, to see how he was doing, and they dutifully spoke. For the first week it was lovely, to be suddenly freed from responsibility. He dressed in sweatpants, and some mornings did not shave. But by the second week—with Jenny in Orgeval, a tiny Paris suburb where business partners of her father lived—it began to seem menacing not to have any place to go. Steven's discipline, as a boy, had always come from somewhere outside: From his parents, then his teachers, then his college advisors, finally, during the last year, the prissy junior editor at the publishing house. His personality had been defined in its response to these various demands. With the demands removed, Steven seemed to have no personality at all.

And though it had seemed playful, at first, for Jenny to bestow this outrageous gift, the act now seemed to queerly weigh upon him. He had traded his love in for something else, for this landlord-tenant relationship. He did his studying, but the Southport landscape never seemed quite real to him. The beauty of the fall—the trees turning their various fierce varieties of red, their leaves twirling down in imitation of the paper helicopters from his arts-and-crafts childhood—was lost on him, found no response behind his eyes. He had considered himself—he'd been an Art History minor—particularly open to beauty. That this landscape shouldn't touch him was worrying.

It was imperative, though, when Jenny came back from Orgeval—first stopping in New York, to give a progress report to her father—that Steven keep up the outward trappings of loyalty. He had two weeks till the exam: It would be too discombobulating to have to move before the test, and he really did feel, in a way, he realized, committed to law school. If he was going to have to be pushed around by people, in his life, it might as well be for a lot of money. The weekend of Jenny's visit to the house was trying. Steven slept with her more out of duty than out of desire—"sing for your supper" had been the thought that kept grimly reasserting itself, during their coupling—and Jenny seemed, distressingly, not to notice, or to enjoy the new arrangement. She'd even come bearing a wrapped gift, which Steven unwrapped: Antique French andirons. "For your new house," she explained, laughing.

The exam was six hours, and by the last week, Steven felt

he'd studied as much as he could. He did not deserve this luxury, was what he decided was disturbing him. The microwave, the many cable movie stations, none of it, none of this smoothness of life belonged to him. It was in Jenny's genes, somehow; someone in her family had acquired it by dint of labor. Steven had acquired it only through seduction, so of course it could not matter. The last week he spent idly flicking through TV stations, watching the New York news, then the Connecticut news, then Cable News Network, as if he were preparing for some mammoth current events quiz.

After the exam—with its pinch of tension, the other people in the room all looking nervous and drawn but on, tingling, in the excited way Steven had missed; the rigmarole with driver's licenses and signatures was also exciting, underlining the seriousness of their enterprise, the group of them all staring down, in this room, at the avenues of their futures, the authorities administering one final check of their identities before letting them run, letting them gallop away— Jenny and Steven and the other girl celebrated, but Steven felt too glum to act happy. He and the girl compared answers, and Jenny gamely tried to involve herself in the questions. He cursed himself, for having said he was jealous to Shelly: this slip of the tongue, this effort to engage—he saw now—the attention of a slightly bored girl had cast him in the role of cold exploiter, from which he now saw no escape. Yet when Jenny, with a wave of her wrist, produced her corporate Gold Card to pay for the meal, Steven felt not the excitement of the exploiter but, somehow, the sad helplessness of the exploited, looking for humor in his plight. The waiter had come with the black tray bearing their check, and something on Steven's face—though the waiter's inclination had clearly been to bring man and bill together— had caused the tray to hover uncertainly, and the waiter to make an interrogative noise with his throat. Jenny went for her purse immediately, and all eyes had, unfortunately, lingered on Steven. He had not, to his dismay, even reached for his wallet. "I've gotten used to living on Fuld benevolence," he said, blood rushing to his face, the tension crumpling into a laugh which the two girls, after a second, shared, and to which even the waiter added, a clear, di-syllabic "Ha, ha." And before this man Steven felt as exposed as he had in the taxi. He felt transparent, and was relieved, when he looked down, that he could not see the tabletop through his demurely folded hands.

October brought with it applications to fill out for his ten law schools, calls to Washington to arrange application fees from his parents. They had been abashed by his move to Southport—he was living, alone, in a house bigger than the Silver Spring one-story they shared—and now didn't even discuss career moves with him, as if he were a glamorous official they'd once voted for whose moves they could only watch, and neither compliment nor condone. This upset Steven. They, too, had given him over to the Fulds. Sitting in an upstairs room—there were so many, each with their hint of naphthalene and harvest of dead flies behind the screen, that it was difficult to decide where to work—Steven could not start his essays. The application question that asked for a curriculum vitae was impossible to answer: What were his likes and dislikes, his enthusiasms and boredoms? He had forgotten them all. He wondered how long Jenny intended to keep him here, or rather, to let him stay. Shelly would already be in school now. He knew he could not go back to his apartment. New York no longer seemed his city: he'd neglected to leave a thread behind him to follow back. It belonged to Jenny, to her large apartment. It was not his to return to.

He called Shelly; she was surprised to hear he was living in Southport, happy he was going to law school. She heard immediately that something was wrong, and asked, and when Steven said "Nothing," divined, "It's living in her house, isn't it? I thought you were ready to leave her months ago. What happened?"

"I don't know. I envied her mobility, I guess. She was always flying to Paris and Rome and Silicon Valley. I guess I just wanted to get moving somewhere too."

"Well," Shelly said, craftily, "you sound stuck to me. You quit, I take it."

"I just couldn't bear it anymore. Every time I made a mistake, Jeffrey would shake his head as if it were a personal affront, as if there were some great tragedy at work that had resulted in graduating students who could leave the 'a' out in 'separate.' I mean, he's only five years older than us, Shelly, and I didn't go to college to learn how to type."

So they were allies; both had failed to measure up to their first jobs, there was a relief in admitting to each other just how much they'd hated their first years; like people brought together by a common friend waiting to gossip, their impressions poured out. Steven was happy to at least hear himself speaking in a humorous way again, to watch his personality reasserting itself. The Robinson Crusoe, Walden Pond thing was a farce, he saw. Crusoe had had a native there to remind him he was European, Thoreau had gone home to have his laundry done. Human beings needed each other, to shape and model them. Shelly was at school in Baltimore, living in a large high-rise. She was sure there were apartments available in her building, she would look into getting one for Steven. The possibility of another escape thrilled him.

The move came a week later, as Shelly called back with information on his new apartment, it's low rent, the probability of jobs in the university area. Steven now saw, as if looking into an abyss, what he would be falling into: his parent's zone of influence, the Chesapeake basin, with its many roads and highways all snaking into octopus Washington. He was leaving behind the good life he'd begun to mine from Jenny, this house, Paris—she'd started mentioning bringing him on trips—Palo Alto. The house now sang to him, but walking through it his last days there, he was unable to manufacture any convincing nostalgia, any pain in his coming departure. It was the possibility of ease in life, the sacrifice of *that*, which pained him. Shelly had asked how the month had been and Steven, again without thinking, had said, "A blur," and, immediately, of course, this was what the month became. A blur of multiple choice studying. In the future, Steven reminded himself, he would have to be more careful of the words with which he colored his past.

He called Jenny after he already had most of his stuff in Baltimore. It was an odd, small city, like Brooklyn in many ways, only friendly and not so second-rate feeling as Brooklyn, without a large city immediately nearby to cower to. He saw her on his trip back to New York, coming in on the Metroliner to break his lease and remove the last few odds and ends—not the futon, God help him, with its sour residue of envious nights—from his Cornelia Street apartment. Jenny, when he met her, refused to handle the situation playfully, was enraged at his departure, his abandonment, enraged at his decision to leave New York which, he cheerfully confessed, was based on her living there. She cried, but in anger. She had exposed something to Steven, her wealth, and he had used it and rejected her at the same time. She had been unfairly treated; he admitted this. She had shown him into her room, it had proven a mistake. Steven explained that as long as he was with her now he couldn't, didn't love her. She had cried, and he had looked down at the menu and read the words, *Onion Rings, $2.75.*

"But I'm too old," she said, and Steven read in her voice not love but pain, at the embarrassing stories she was going to have to tell, at the exposures she was going to have to make to her father and mother about the miscalculation she'd made. Her father, Steven thought, would never had made such an investment without much clearer contracts, without many decisive meetings and more promising telephone conversations. He saw, in the future, that Jenny was going to be tougher. But he was happy to have had this effect on her, happy to have brought her down from the world of airplanes, from her easy, skimming life.

And it was only weeks later, filling out forms in his Baltimore apartment, staring out his window at the fall trees—fall stayed longer in the more southern climate, as the South with its famous hospitality prolonged each season—which he could now see because he was paying for them, that Steven realized everything he had missed, everything he had forfeited. He had paid for the property after all, not with money, but with love.

GARDEN

IN THE YEAR AFTER they graduated from college, all of Leonard's friends, to one degree or another, began to be struck by premonitions of mortality. They had all been raised on ceremony, to expect life to be a passage of doorways: grammar school to a good high school, high school to a good college, college to a good job. Now there were no more doorways, just a wide room, an empty, dim room, with at the end one black doorway leading nowhere at all. It was against this doorway that Leonard's friends seemed to be stumbling all year long. While Leonard, a graduate student, studied English at Georgetown, closing books and then mounting them on his bookcase as if in a display of difficult prey bagged, his friends collapsed. Michael, his hallmate in college, called late one night. He was having a heart attack. He was dying. Leonard lay on his futon, the phone against his cheek, imagining long wires stretching to Los Angeles, Michael's heart attack scurrying across darkened wheat fields to Iowa, Kansas, Ohio, Pennsylvania, Pennsylvania Avenue, here. "Can you feel your heart?" he asked.

"Of course I can feel it," his friend said. "I feel it in my ears, my shoulders, my muscles. It's all I *can* feel. I don't know what to do."

"Count the number of beats," Leonard said, and was surprised to hear, in his voice, the instructions he'd received from his Chaucer professor for telling the difference between strophe and anapestic meter. "I'll give you a minute on my watch, you count the number of beats. Okay?" Leonard held up his wrist, so streetlight could illuminate the dial. "Go."

Michael's count was 85—nowhere near, Leonard knew, a heart attack. Michael was nervous, home in California without a job. Leonard told him to call a doctor in the morning.

But other calls came, too—his friends seemed to think Leonard was stable, back in the hallway with more doors to open, and thus capable of giving unhysterical advice. But Leonard found that even among his fellow graduate students, life-threatening diseases were rampant. One friend worried about brain tumors, another about the pattern of moles on her arm. A friend from high school now at Columbia checked himself into Payne Whitney for a night, and stayed for a month. Leonard, beginning work on a long paper in March and coming down with the worst cold he'd had since the fourth grade, decided two things: that he would flee Georgetown, and that he had AIDS.

He handled the first problem directly. He called Michael in Los Angeles. Michael would be moving to New York in April, to start work at the magazine owned by a friend of his father's. Leonard would be leaving Georgetown the following month. Would Michael mind finding an apartment for both of them?

The second problem attacked Leonard in two ways. He tried to decide how he'd gotten the disease, and came up with a woman he'd met playing tennis one summer, a tall, beautiful

Asian who was uncertain of herself in the way tall pretty women sometimes are, as if their beauty and height are stilts they're afraid the first mean person will topple them from. She was twenty-eight, and Leonard, twenty, had slept with her, feeling it a sort of victory. He'd felt handsome that summer for the first time in his life. That this woman (twenty-eight! from Harvard! in investment banking!) would sleep with him so casually seemed a welcome from the adult world, which he had then imagined as glamorous and powerful. The woman had complained of a previous lover, a ballet dancer who had been cruel to her. To Leonard, in March, "cruel" now seemed a euphemism for sodomy, and this woman, who had been so welcoming, now seemed to have welcomed him to something else, to the area behind the black door in that dim, empty room. Each morning, when he woke, he checked his arms for dots, for suspicious marks. He began wearing sweatshirts to avoid this morning performance, and found himself sweating in his sleep. Nightsweats were a symptom. In the shower, avoiding the sight of his unfurled skin, Leonard found himself praying.

This was the second dimension Leonard's sense of the disease took: he believed that if he prayed, if he behaved rightly, he would be spared. The disease was a way of keeping him in line, keeping him from feeling too happy or satisfied with himself. In the fall, as his postgraduate friends, pursuing jobs in Manhattan, had spats, fell apart, checked in with neurologists, heart specialists, and sleep therapists, Leonard had found himself enjoying Georgetown, loving it in a way he never had college. The smoky smell that hung in the streets—from fireplaces that actually worked—the candy-colored row houses, all the same height, the *swish-swish* of trees overhead, these things had made Leonard feel adult, and thrilled with life. He'd left the girl he'd dated in

college, and had taken up with another girl, an undergraduate in the section of one of his friends. When the ex-
girlfriend called, tentatively proposing reconciliation,
Leonard had felt safe on a high, happy perch, looking down
on avoided misery. AIDS was his punishment for happiness.
He broke up with the undergraduate, and reconciled with
the original girl. He began to keep kosher, which struck him
as a small sacrifice. And he began to limit his conversation to
assertions of whether things were good or better—to be
critical was to risk extermination.

This caused problems. He couldn't say no to people. When
Michael called and proposed he pay rent for April also, since
the apartment (a first-floor tenement on West 20th Street,
with a garden) was for his use as well, Leonard argued
vehemently. Michael said, "I can't believe we're arguing.
I'm here in this apartment because you needed a place to
come back to. I'm not even asking you to pay the full rent,
though I could just as easily have stayed in California."

"You told me you were going crazy in California,"
Leonard reminded him. "You called me on the phone and
told me you were having a heart attack."

Leonard could feel Michael registering this. It was taboo to
talk about that evening; for a moment, Leonard feared his
friend would hang up. "In any event," Michael said with a
nasty click in his voice, "I'm here, in this apartment, which
is rented in both our names, because you asked me to be.
And I'm not paying the first month's rent alone."

They fought for an hour, coming to no special conclusion,
and when Leonard got off the phone he panicked. What had
he been thinking? Was it worth five hundred dollars to die?
He carefully rolled back the sleeve of his shirt to look at his
forearm. The red dots, which had seemed to be gone that
morning, now were pulsing as brightly and happily as ever.

In the morning he sneezed, twice, he coughed, his pee seemed frothier than usual. In the shower he dared examine both arms and felt about to cry, the dots were there, when he looked. He prayed. And then, when he got out of the shower, he called New York, leaving a message on Michael's answering machine. "Sorry about last night, and anything I may have said. I was tense about leaving Georgetown. Of course I'll pay my half of the rent. See you Friday." And then, hanging up, he'd felt terrible.

Next was Alexa, his old girlfriend. She was looking forward to his return to the city. She called and asked if he wouldn't mind helping paint her apartment. What could Leonard say?

It was the first of May, and scorching in the early Washington summer, the day Leonard left Georgetown. On the Amtrak next to him was a tidily dressed businessman with many magazines. Leonard asked to borrow *Sports Illustrated*. His seatmate gave it to him with an edgy expression, the look of a man clearly pained by the idea of someone else's getting something for nothing. Leonard read. He felt he was unlikely to be ambushed here by medical information, and he hoped the bland scores and sports photographs would calm him down. But the sports information and his AIDS thoughts were in a race in his head, and in the end AIDS outpaced *Sports Illustrated*, tackled it to the ground and jumped up and down on top of it, trumpeting victory. Leonard returned the magazine. His seatmate took it, then tore it in half. For the rest of the trip, each time this man finished a magazine, he would look at Leonard and tear it first into halves, then into quarters, dropping the remains to the carpet under his feet. At Penn Station, Leonard hailed a taxi, got in, and gave detailed directions. His driver swiveled in his seat. "Relax," he said. "You've found a driver who's white and speaks English. You've hit the jackpot." In their apartment, Michael was sitting in the living room, taking his own blood pressure.

"Shh," he said, pumping the bulb. When he was finished, he showed Leonard the kitchen, the closets, the bedroom. Then he took him outside to the garden. It was lovely. There were two chairs and a barrel table. Dark clouds moved across an even darker sky. There were herbs and birds, and even the many weeds were handsome and fresh-smelling. A cool breeze came up from the west, drying the sweat on Leonard's forehead. He pictured himself here in summer, in winter. "Is it all ours?" he asked.

Michael nodded, pulling out one of the chairs. "There's a priest on the second floor who keeps wanting to plant things. Apparently, the last tenant let him keep his own flower bed."

"Should we let him?" Leonard asked.

"Of course not," Michael said, sitting down. His upper arm was still red, from where the blood pressure apparatus had been wrapped around it. He had the Californian's matter-of-fact cruelty, which to Leonard seemed to come from learning to view human accidents not as catastrophes, but as inconveniences which tied up the freeway. "We probably pay five times the rent he does. If he wants a garden, let him find another apartment. He certainly can't use ours."

Waking, on the floor, in the living room, in Michael's sleeping bag—Michael had taken the bedroom; this was only fair, he'd explained, since he'd found the apartment—Leonard realized he could not go on. He had thought he couldn't face the AIDS exam. Now, though, he grabbed for the White Pages, and called the number for Department of

Health HIV Information. A recorded voice came on and told him to wait, first in English, then in Spanish. Then radio music came on, exactly as though this were a department store he'd called, or some other cheery place. The first song was "Tonight's the Night." The second was "Dust in the Wind." Leonard slammed the phone down. Were they kidding? He didn't think he could face, this morning, the shower, the menacing, unexplored territory of his own skin. He pulled on shorts, a shirt, and ran out the door.

In the hallway, a man in a priest's outfit was getting his mail. Leonard's back stiffened. All spring long, he had been especially nice to clergymen. It didn't even matter what denomination—if Leonard behaved correctly, they were bound to put in a good word for him with the agency for which they worked. He tried to slip past, but the man looked up and said, "Ahh, you must be Leonard. I'm Father Halliday." Father Halliday was in his sixties, bald, with rapidly blinking eyes and ears folded up intricately against his skull, like bat's wings. He inclined his head, and spoke in a confiding, slightly effeminate voice: "Now, Michael told me to take this up with you, he said you were the gardener. I'm a gardener, too, and as he may have mentioned, I have the most beautiful zinnias and begonias which I could plant in your garden, to give it a little color. What do you say?"

"I'd love to talk about it right now, but I'm late, I'm very sorry." Leonard kept moving. He didn't dare check his arms. And, on Eighth Avenue, he didn't dare look at the little cluster of newspaper machines comparing headlines under a lamppost. In Georgetown, he had measured his moral progress by the number of *Washington Post* articles dealing with AIDS. The better he acted, the fewer there were likely to be. On the subway, a swaying woman told a rambling story about her abusive, jailbird husband, as preamble to

asking for money. Other riders—competitors? critics?—
heckled her, for delivery and general believability. Leonard
gave a dollar. It was a moral toll charge. Alexa was waiting
in her apartment on Perry Street. They kissed. Alexa was a
tall, slim girl with arching eyebrows. She—solo in Leonard's
acquaintance—had gone through the year unscathed by
disease. She'd been unscathed by anything. She'd started the
summer working for one magazine and, finding it boring,
had switched in midwinter to another. Disliking the Upper
East Side, she'd moved down here. She was the sort of
person who scented out what she wanted and then zeroed
unswervingly in after it, like a hunting dog. She had zeroed
in on Leonard, at Georgetown. Now, she was zeroing in on
giving her apartment a new coat of white.

As they painted—a sharp smell, rollers spraying up paint
against their forearms and faces—Leonard couldn't help
examining Alexa's arms and legs for dots and other telltale
markings. That she could work so aggressively, with no hint
at all of the terrible battle that might even then be raging
within her (plucky white blood cells versus hordes of
invading virus), made Alexa seem innocently brave. They
painted in silence, one or the other of them occasionally
journeying into the kitchen to change the radio station.
Alexa seemed irritated. After two hours, she said, testily,
"Leonard. I wish you wouldn't keep staring at me that
way."

He asked, "What way?"

"Like you wish I were somebody else." Alexa swung
around to face him. The ends of her hair were flecked with
Glidden Spred Satin, there was a fine dusting of white spots
over her cheekbones, like freckles. Her eyes were narrowed,
and her nostrils were dilating and shrinking, as they did
when she scented outrage. "What do you want me to say,

Leonard? I'm sorry I asked you to paint my apartment! I'm
sorry I'm not your little freshman friend from Georgetown!"

"She was a junior," Leonard said, timorously. He felt that
if he stuck to the facts, he would stay blameless.

Alexa advanced, stepping over paint cans and the
aluminum-foil roller tray. She put her hands on her hips.
"And how you could sleep with one of your own students I
can never understand, either."

She was one of my friend's students, Leonard wanted to
say. But with Alexa so close—so close that he could smell
her, anger, and sweat, and (vaguely) perfume, and paint—
he was dazzled by the planes of exposed skin now revealed
to him: collarbone, earlobes, jawline, there was so much
territory to cover! Alexa's face contracted and expanded in
disbelief. "See? You're doing it right now!"

What she couldn't understand was that he was monitoring
his behavior by her condition. "Let's not talk about this right
now," he said.

"Why not? We have to talk about this. How can we ever
stay together if we can't even talk to each other?" And
Leonard understood; Alexa had zeroed in on marriage. The
CD ended. Alexa, in her excess of anger, whirled into the
kitchen, as if her stereo, too, had failed her. Leonard
dropped his roller and walked out of the apartment.

His stomach was jumping all over the place. He began to
walk uptown, towards his apartment. The presence of so
many people on the street made Leonard feel less special,
and thus less afraid. Taking a deep breath, he looked down
at his arms. They were covered with splotches. White, the
hair matted. It was paint. But it was how the disease would
look. Leonard took another deep breath. He tried to remember how he'd felt in Georgetown, in the fall, with the other
girl, the wood smells, his own ease. It seemed a paradise

he'd been ejected from. Acquired immune deficiency syndrome. It was iambic pentameter. Recognizing this calmed him down, some.

He would have to become cruel. This, he saw, was the solution. God, perhaps, required that you be loving, and nice, but the world required cruelty and indifference. Leonard thought of the racist cab driver, the man on the Amtrak, the passengers on the subway, even Michael and Alexa. They were all at home making demands, acting selfishly, withholding things. If you were not cruel, Leonard decided, people would get anything out of you they wanted. You were a door with no locks, waiting to be ransacked. And this information, itself, seemed another doorway through which Leonard was passing.

At 20th Street he turned. Father Halliday was waiting on the sidewalk, in front of their building. As Leonard approached, he took a breath, and his eyes seemed to visibly consider strategies, and Leonard, panicking, head down, cut him off saying, "Yes, yes, yes: please use our garden."

MARCH 1, 1987

I'T'S ELEVEN-FIFTEEN, and Michael is jogging. It rained during the day, and he's being careful to avoid stepping in puddles. Still, the bottoms of his shoes are wet, and when his feet kick up, a fine muddy spray impacts against the backs of his thighs. It's the first of March. This hits Michael in a funny way, as he jogs. He's used to seeing things in series: Tuesday, for instance, as a bridge between Monday and Wednesday. Actually, that it rained today is the most recent event in human history. Michael is moving at the farthest point the planet has yet reached, on the tip, running into the future.

He is trying to decide whether or not he should run over to Amanda's house. He had a fight with her, earlier. Friday, she'd thrown a party at her house; Saturday, she'd gone home—her grandmother was turning ninety, the sort of party Michael thinks is eminently missable—and Sunday, on her return, she'd called him. They began talking about Friday's party. Michael talked along for a few minutes, until it occurred to him that the conversation was so dull it was staggering. Amanda was talking about how, luckily, most of the popcorn she'd prepared had successfully popped. Michael laughed harshly. "I can't believe we're talking about popping versus unpopping kernels." Amanda was silent. Michael said, "I mean, if you want to check in with me, tell me you're back from your grandmother's, that's fine. But for God's sake, to talk about popcorn kernels over the telephone." Amanda said that she wouldn't waste any more of his time, and hung up the phone.

Amanda has an art history exam in the morning, and Michael knows that if he doesn't apologize tonight, she will blame him for any difficulties tomorrow. "Well, I was just so angry," she'll say. He won't have to apologize in words, anyway. Just being in Amanda's room will be apology enough, for he jogs over to her house this late only when they've had a fight. As long as he's home by midnight. Michael's glasses begin to fog, from the heat rising from his cheeks. He can't see. He takes them off and holds them in his hand, thumb on the lens. Without his glasses, the world looks starry and soft-edged—objects like lampposts seem as if they would be not painful to run into but forgivingly embracing, like foam rubber. When Michael sees a car, though—the slithering sound, the dark, slippery shadow, the two bright lights—he knows to get out of the street, and this is what counts.

Amanda lives in a house with three other women, in an area populated mostly by students. Most of the richer kids at school don't live on campus. It isn't even that living off campus is more expensive—it's a matter of style, a way to set yourself apart, and also to have enough closet space for ski boots and the original packing material of digital stereo equipment.

He does a few stretches outside Amanda's door after he rings the bell (the icy button leaving a little indentation in the ball of his thumb). First he leans against the wall and stretches out the backs of his calves—he imagines gummy bow strings being pulled taut. Then he spreads his legs and leans first to one side, then to the other, the bands in his hamstrings sweetly aching. When Jill comes to the screen door she finds him in this ridiculous pose. "Michael?" she says. Michael loves her voice. There is always an icy, jokey trickle, as if behind everything she says there lies a subtext of hundreds of more telling remarks she could have selected— even when, as now, this cannot really be the case: "You can come in now, if you want to."

He laughs, in sheer joy. "I'm just stretching," he says. He stands up straight, clownishly rotates an ankle till it cracks. "There," he says. "I'm stretched." Jill smiles and opens the door for him. He walks into the warm entryway, where he can hear the gargling *swish-swish* of the dishwasher.

"Amanda's upstairs," Jill says. "I think she's gone to sleep."

Michael tries to tell from her voice whether Amanda has mentioned their fight. He looks down at his foggy glasses, debates whether to put them on. He would have worn his contacts, only they're back in his room, drifting in a bath of fizzy enzyme cleaner. It's always hard for him to think of things to say to Jill. "I hear you guys had some butcher trouble on Friday," he says.

"Hm?" Jill asks. "Oh, yes. Amanda found it before she went home. She said it was really disgusting." The morning after their party, Amanda went downstairs and found a ceramic bowl on the table. Inside were cow's intestines and pig's feet. Amanda had no idea who'd left the bowl.

"I always feel, whenever anyone tells me something like that, that what they're really doing is waiting for me to confess." Michael experiences a little thrill, saying this; any intimacy he reveals to her can only knit them closer.

Jill laughs. "It means you either have a guilty conscience

193

or you're doing something wrong and are afraid of being caught." Michael steps aside and Jill goes into the kitchen. She opens the refrigerator door, unflinchingly accepting its bright light, and kneels down to sift through the fruit-and-vegetable drawer like an actress receiving a bouquet on stage.

Michael runs upstairs. He opens the door that leads to the second flight, then runs up these stairs to Amanda's bedroom. In the dark hallway, it takes him a moment to find her doorknob, his hand bumping over the wood. Stepping into her room, he begins to sweat. He always starts sweating about five minutes after jogging, a delayed reaction, his laggard pores getting the message only much too late. Amanda's bedroom is less dark than the hall. She's under her comforter. Her clock—a big red digital, with numbers three inches high, mocking the very idea of clocks—says 11:34. Amanda stirs, a lump under the pale flowered quilt. "Hi," she says, in her sleepy voice. "I thought it was you."

Michael is glad she can't see him with his glasses. He knows he doesn't look good with them. He puts them down on the bookcase and sits on the bed.

"Hi," he says. He can hear his own voice taking on something of her sleepy, whispering warmth. Her room is very warm. "I was jogging."

"I know it," Amanda says. Michael looks at her face. He loves how small it is, its sharpness. Amanda has her eyes closed, and a little smile. He loves her most when she is like this, asleep or near sleep. He feels then as if the barriers that separate them during the day are gone, they can become shiftily closer, like the lamppost seen with his glasses off. He touches her face, moving his fingers along her cheek. It is warm and soft, with fine traces of down. When his fingers come near her lips, she kisses them.

194

"Did your sister find me gallant and charming?" Amanda's sister came down from Boston for the party. Michael spent the party passing her witty anecdotes like hors d'oeuvres, slandering the other party guests, standing with her by the bright steel bowl of popcorn. Essentially, he considers, Amanda had been within her rights to talk about the popcorn, since he'd eaten most of it and it had in fact been popped with him in mind.

"Mm-hmm," Amanda hums.

"What did she say? Did she say she found me charming?"

"She said you told her about all the people I didn't introduce her to."

"That's right," Michael says. His T-shirt is becoming soggy, at the neck and armpits. Amanda rolls over. She is wearing a T-shirt which says, "Mount Holyoke Crew: Eight Fast Women and a Cox." Mount Holyoke is the school she transferred from. Her pajama bottoms are green. Michael bought her a pair of L. L. Bean red ones for Christmas. Usually, she wears these. When they fight, she wears the green ones.

"It's funny," he says, putting his fingertips on her chin. "From this angle, you look just like your sister." He gently turns her face the other way. "But from this side, you look just like Grace Kelly."

Amanda makes a laughing sound with her nose. "Right. I don't remember Grace Kelly having brown hair."

"Oh, but she did, actually," Michael lies. "You have her exact features." Amanda repeats her laugh, but Michael knows he has hit on one of the things that most attracts him to her. She is *exactly* like Grace Kelly: rich, remote, beautiful, though this is probably not the way she would describe herself.

Amanda leans forward and kisses the backs of his fingers.

195

He moves his hand from her chin and touches the front of her hair, still stiff from the mousse she uses to set it. Sweat makes a plopping sound as it drops from his forehead onto her pillowcase. Amanda says, "I've been indoors all day," and begins describing preparations for her exam. Michael only half listens. While she is talking, he leans over her face and rubs his wet forehead against her warm one. When he is finished, he turns and rubs his cheek against hers. Then he tilts his head and rubs his other cheek against her other one. Finally, he swabs her chin with his; he feels like an Apache, rubbing a fellow Indian's features with war paint. "Sweaty," Amanda says, without protest.

"I know you didn't get a chance to run, so I'm trying to make you feel as if you had."

"Thanks," she says. "Was it cold outside?"

"Not too. But then I was jogging, so it was hard to tell."

He runs the tip of his sweaty nose down the length of hers, then punctuates this by kissing her lips. "Hey," she says.

He looks at the clock. He wants to be home by midnight. "I have to go," he says. It's 11:45. "I just stopped over to say hello."

"Where do you have to go?" Amanda asks, locking an arm behind his neck.

"Home," he says. "I have to go home."

"Rub my back first?" She flips over, kicking her legs out from beneath the comforter. Michael reaches under her filmy T-shirt and runs his hand over the warm expanse of her back.

After a few minutes he taps her shoulders, meaning he's finished rubbing. "I have to go," he repeats. It's 11:49. Amanda arches her neck up and he kisses her cheek. She shakes her head: "Uh-uh." He leans over and kisses her lips. "Mmm," she says. He gets up and picks up his glasses.

"Good luck tomorrow," he says.

"Thank you," Amanda says.

He goes back downstairs. Jill's door is closed. He can hear music coming from inside—Sade, the slow, languorous, West African beat. He knocks on the door and Jill says, "Come in." She's sitting at her Macintosh, with its smart-aleck gangster expression, its little mouth set over to one side. There are a lot of open books on her desk. She holds up a finger and says, "Just a minute," and Michael listens to the plunk-plunk of her typing. He can still feel Amanda's back under his fingertips; the way his pores forget to sweat, his neurons, nicely, seem sometimes to forget to stop firing a signal. Jill gets up and turns around. She's wearing a green turtleneck jersey and black, loose-fitting pants, Middle Eastern somehow. She looks like an amalgamation of all the girls he didn't date in high school.

She says, "How's Amanda?"

"Fine," Michael says. "Sleeping." He thinks of something to say to her. "Have you heard from the *Times?*"

Jill shakes her head. That she has applied for a job at the *Times* is one of the house's many non-secrets. "Not yet." The glittery twinkle again.

"Well," Michael says, picking up one of her books— Foucault's *Madness and Civilization*—reading the dust jacket and putting it back down again, her place reverently retained, "I'm sure that's a good sign. We all wrote letters in to the editor last week saying 'Please Hire Jill'—you might have seen them on the Op-Ed page—so I'm sure you'll get it."

Jill laughs. The truth is that Michael first came into this house to court Jill. It was a year and a half ago. Jill had not been interested; she'd been dating a wealthy boy from Peru, whose problems—failure to graduate, a soft spot for drugs— made him much more interesting than Michael ever could be.

He doesn't want to risk saying something unfunny after making Jill laugh; he puts on his glasses. Jill looks at him; he can feel her wondering whether to ask about his own job prospects—he hopes she won't—but one of the unspoken rules of senior year is that you don't ask someone what they're doing vis-à-vis jobs unless they've already volunteered information. Truthfully, Michael doesn't know what he is doing next year—about Amanda (the secret cause of all their fights this spring), about jobs, about anything. His future is a big black circle he has been running around all year. Jill says, "You can sit down, if you want," indicating a sling chair by her bed, but Michael looks at her clock and sees its 11:55. "I have to go," he says. He says good-bye and runs downstairs, outside. The cold air and stars sting his face.

Walking in this air—much colder than when he was jogging—he thinks about Jill's job. He's sure she'll get the position, he'll see her many years from now, on the street somewhere, glamorously dressed. She's already fallen into the tug of a television-perfect life, is being shuttled along towards an ideal adulthood, while Michael has been fighting the pull of the opposite, messier world. He will never kiss her. His life will be an increasing series of nevers. He starts jogging again. He sprints home. The street is empty. He runs down the center, seeing how fast he can go. Running down Thayer, he watches the slow figures moving in Zab's Backyard Hots, the hands of the huge antique clock pinching two minutes between them. By the time he is back in his room he is winded, and has to stretch again. But he isn't sweating.

His room, too, is dark. He switches on a light, undresses. It's cold. In his underwear, he kneels down over his radiator—feeling the heat on his face, even on his eyes—and turns it up to full blast. Even then, it's cold in his room. He goes to his dresser (brushing sandy grit from his knees) and takes out the sweatshirt which says "Penn Crew." It belonged to Amanda's brother—Michael had liked it, so she'd given it to him. He decides not to go downstairs to brush his teeth. It will be fine to brush them in the morning.

In bed, the lights off, he looks out the window. It's at the end of his room, and looks out over the whole city. It's the real reason he lives on campus; he loves this view. It's gray out, but still light. He slides his legs under his blanket and sheet, trying to make the bed less tight. He reaches up and picks up his clock, to set the alarm. It is a red box that runs on batteries, with a little gray window. When he presses a button on top, a light comes on so he can read the time. It is just after midnight—March 2, 1987. He sets the alarm for seven-fifty. He likes the idea of this clock waking him. His mother bought it his first year at school, the day they arrived, at the campus bookstore. Neither of them had known then, four years earlier, what school would be like, what would happen to him, how he would turn out. The alarm had gone off his first morning, and would go off again now. He puts it back on his dresser and settles deeper under the covers. He still has his glasses on. He lifts them off. The view grows fuzzy, the rest of his room wavers. He puts them back on. Growing up, he spent hundreds of evenings at sleep-overs—the clock-radio on, his own voice talking, the shadows of leaves drifting across the ceiling in yellow frames of streetlight. Thinking about this makes him unwilling to take off his glasses. In those years, his eyesight had been perfect, and lying in bed before sleep, talking about girls or what he would do as an adult, the feeling he'd had was identical to the one he had the day he bought the clock with his mother, that he was a boy of infinite promise, in a world of infinite possibility.

SPRINGS, 1977

IT IS THE SUMMER OF 1977, and I am in Springs, East Hampton, with my two sons, Walter and Peter. I am thirty-five, somewhat attractive, and divorced. Peter and Walter are thirteen and eleven. For the past ten months they've been living with their father in Connecticut. I'm trying to make the most of the summer—three months— though I know this will only make it worse when they return to Hartford, which they'll do the first of September.

This morning, the first of August, as Peter and I walk out to the station wagon, the air is chilly, for the first time in weeks. It's as if the weather is consciously reminding us of the tough times to come. When Peter opens the door and throws our towels into the backseat, he steps into the shadow of a tree, and, watching him suppress a shiver, I have to suppress my own urge to hug him, or to order him into the house for a sweatshirt. But I've never wanted to be that kind of mother. Peter slams the door, and is embarrassed to find me staring at him. "Walter says it's getting over eighty today," he says.

I nod. We've come to depend on him in his new role: Walter as weatherman. He doesn't come to the beach with us anymore. He and Peter biked into town last week to see *Jaws* (they show it at the same theater all summer, a cruel trick to play on parents spending many thousands of dollars to be by the ocean), and Walter came back with the resolute look of a smoker who has just received his first lecture on the dangers of lung cancer. He was named by my ex-husband after the famous newscaster, as a kind of joke, since, as a baby, he was always so quiet and solemn. The name stuck—one of the reasons I got divorced—and, to be honest, it's had its advantages. Where Peter's lunch bags and cubbyholes have always read "Peter F.," Walter has remained, sublimely, himself, without identifying initial. On the other hand, Walter has always seemed preternaturally attracted to television, actually talented at watching it. While we are at the beach he juggles four or five shows at once, keeping them aloft in his mental air. I tried forcing him to come with us, but when I did he just sat in the locked car, munching sandwiches, staring out at the ocean like a soldier in a bunker watching for the first advance of enemy infantry.

Peter and I go inside, say good-bye to him, pull on shirts, and get back into the car. It's already warming up, though the ribbed vinyl is cool under my legs. We roll out of our driveway, Peter rolls down his window and rests his forearm on the lip of glass, his flesh pillowing on either side. "It's a beautiful day," I say, swinging a right on Accabonic. "What beach do you want to hit?"

This is the big question of the summer. There are three beaches in East Hampton. We have a sticker that allows us to park at one of them, but it's the one the kids like least—the one I like best, a little bay with flat sunshine and breezes, where you have to stand on tiptoe when one of the frequent, bristling crabs swaggers by—and I don't mind risking the five-dollar ticket to park at the others.

The truth is, the vacation is not working out. My father died last fall, and the money from his life insurance has gone directly into our house, our station wagon, our triple membership (though only Peter is good) at the Dunes Racquet Club. We're spending so much money that I can't bear to open my bank statement when it arrives. I thought the vacation would make the boys happy, and the seaside entice them to move back in with me. To be honest, I conceived of the vacation, sitting alone in my apartment in May, as a kind of advertisement for what living with me would be like. Instead, Walter sits in his room watching television, and Peter, my athletic, blond, handsome son, plays tennis with strangers at the Dunes. I keep trying to do memorable things with them, like taking them to watch shooting stars on the beach. But Walter, without the minimal question-and-answer suspense of his television crime shows, fell asleep staring at the disappointing bowl of the sky. To him, it must have seemed like a balky television refusing to go on. I tried pointing out the constellations I knew to Peter—Orion's Belt, the Big and Little Dippers, twin cooking utensils of the sky—but he seemed more interested in the teenagers who were conducting a sort of pickup truck rodeo on the sand a few hundred yards away. My ex-husband sends the boys postcards from Europe, where he's traveling with his new wife, postcards which he must know I'll read and which all contain the same, mocking variant of "Things are great, wish you were here." I've been keeping these from the boys: if the vacation is going to work, it has to work without interruption from their father. The postcards sit in a pile on my windowsill, next to two fat envelopes from Chase Manhattan, the Louvre and London Bridge and the David, all warping in the sun.

"Maidstone," Peter says. "I told Alex we'd meet him and his father there, if it's okay."

"It's fine," I say. "I just hope we can find a parking space." We pass the revolutionary graveyard, where even now people are out taking photographs of the oldest stones. What a funny thing, to be a tourist in a graveyard! We drive through town, past the ice cream stores and the little sign that says "East Hampton, Voted One of the Five Prettiest Towns in America, 1976."

Alex Colton and his sister go to the same school Peter and Walter used to attend. It's a progressive school, which means that most of the kids come from divorced families, which also means that the staff-psychologist-to-student ratio is one to four. Alex and Samantha are staying with their father and his girlfriend in the lopsided house Sidney Colton designed himself. It's in Springs, pretty near us. I've always liked Sidney. As we park, I slide my eyes up to the mirror, to see how I look, and I look just like me, only hopeful. The parking lot is beginning to get that pleasant stink asphalt gets in the sun. "Which way are we going?" I ask.

Peter looks around. "Alex said they'd be to the right of the lifeguard. They have to go pretty far out, because of the dog."

It's a long walk. Peter drags the raft himself, by its white string. There are black pods all over the sand, and other things, dried, tangled seaweed (rejected film stock) and small crab claws which have been dyed beautiful speckled pinks by the sun. When Alex sees us coming, he waves from the water and Peter goes running to meet him, his raft making a balloony sound as it skims over the sand. Sidney Colton gets up, dusts off his bottom, and walks over to give me a hand. He's wearing the boxy, hide-your-shape trunks most men his age wear, whereas Peter and Alex—who don't even have anyone to show their shapes to—are both wearing Mark Spitz Speedos. Still, I can see the little rounded nub at the groin, where the cloth softly rolls around. Up close, Sidney looks like a Jewish pirate—deep-set, heavy-browed blue eyes, a wide mustache. His son, splashing out of the water, carries himself with similar confidence. Only Alex's chipped front tooth gives any indication of the hard time I know he's had, his parents' breakup, his mother's subsequent alcoholism and breakdown.

"I see you guys made it," he says to Peter, snapping some water out of his ear. His hair is wet, and this is what his personality is like: a damp curl, always ready to spring back up.

Peter and Alex run into the water, and Sidney takes half my things and sets them down on his blanket. I set down the other half. The dog, a big black poodle and cause of our long walk, is sleeping nearby. His side swells up and down, periodically.

Sitting down, Sidney asks, "How's your summer going?" I'm tempted to tell him that the high point was the New York City blackout, when my mother—secretly thrilled by the idea of any family member being in danger—called to make sure everyone was all right. I told her we were fine, there'd been no looting at Dean & DeLuca, the lights in Springs were all still on.

"Fun," I say. "You?" I shrug off my shirt, and I can feel—just feel—a sort of extra blink as Sidney responds to my shoulders.

He shrugs. "I've been in the city most of the time; this next month is my real vacation. Cynthia"—Cynthia is his live-in girlfriend, of five years' good standing—"can still only come out on weekends." He holds out his hands, the backs. "Look: I've got a city tan." He points up to his neck, to the flesh between a phantom collar and his hair, where there is also a band of brownness. "The chains of the working class!" he jokes, though he's in fact an architect.

My own skin is a deep brown—I'm a painter during the year, and this summer it seems like I've been endlessly mixing this one color. It's hard to think of things to say to Sidney, and I've forgotten the rhythm of heterosexual adult conversation, the charged advance and retreat. It would be easier for me to be parental, to point out that he's left a dollopy smear of suntan lotion in the hair on his chest, or that if he doesn't put something on his nose, it'll be peeling by the weekend.

So instead of talking, I locate our own bottle of suntan lotion. I squirt a little into my palm and begin spreading it out over my arms and legs. Sand gets mixed in, adding a nice grittiness to the project. Sidney shifts his position, which means he's watching, since it's the kind of thing you only remember to do when you're being nonchalant. A year and a half ago, when the boys still lived in the city, we had dinner together after a parent-faculty meeting at the school. Sidney told me he liked me, that he and Cynthia were splitting, and that he wanted to see me again. I gave him my number, but he never called.

Peter and Alex come splashing out of the water. The dog gets excited, running alongside them, and barks. Sidney looks guiltily towards the other end of the beach. Peter and Alex have that salty sea smell. They plunk down and start eating. Peter picks up his sandwich, bites in, and accuses me of applying too much mayonnaise. Alex asks, "Want to play Kadima?" It's the rage of the summer, an Israeli game involving clownishly large paddles and a small, hard, dark rubber ball. The idea is to keep this ball in the air as long as possible. It's nice to see they've finally invented noncompetitive games for boys.

I look at Sidney, and he lifts his eyebrows. I can't think of anything to say, so I smile dreamily and turn over on my stomach. Alex comes back and says, "Dad, you play. I'm wiped out." Sidney looks at me, gets up, and plays. Because he knows I'm watching, he plays with extra intensity—the swim trunks don't hide the fact that his legs are muscular, or that when he moves, he moves gracefully. He makes Peter run all over, catching his shots in the sand, returning lobs. Being from my generation, he has converted the game into at least a semi-competitive one. Alex, meanwhile, collapses next to me. The dog comes over and lies down between us, sphinxlike, mouth open, pink tongue moving in and out.

Sidney and Peter return to our enclave, chests heaving. We all get up to leave. The lifeguard, from his perch of moral rectitude, scowls down at the dog as we walk by. The asphalt is now too hot to stand on, and the cars parked there, with their shiny metal and their windows each reflecting a slice of sun, are too bright to look at. From the door of his green Volvo, Sidney calls, "Be seeing you," and drives off.

Safe in our own car, the doors open like wings to allow the interior to cool, Peter complains, "Mom, did you see the way Sidney was playing? Does he always take sports so seriously?"

"I don't think he really understands the game," I say. Once again, we have not gotten a ticket. I say a little silent thank-you to the members of the East Hampton Police Department, and we back out of the lot.

Back home, Wally gives us the day's news wrap-up and brings us up-to-date as to what's been happening on the soaps. Peter changes into tennis gear and bikes over to the Dunes. Walter tells me, "I finished another scene." Our secret—Peter isn't supposed to know—is that he's been writing a screenplay all summer, often while he watches television. It's about detectives in outer space, and is subtitled, *An NBC Sunday Night Movie*. He's the first person I've ever known to write directly for television. When we were married, my ex-husband decided he wanted to be a writer. He took a year off from his law office to finish a screenplay. Throughout this period, I supported him with my sales. The screenplay—*Double Life, Double Wife*—was about a man who quits his job as a lawyer and makes his wife support him through prostitution. When I read this, I immediately demanded he go back to work again. Walter's screenplay has become a medium through which we communicate. Neither of the boys will tell me much about their new life in Hartford. But in the play, the detectives live on a suburban planet called Confordia, which bears a suspicious resemblance to Connecticut ("All the spaceships are made on other planets," one of the set directions says). Often, as now, when we sit down to go over what he's written, I feel a tiny space between Wally and me, a kind of barrier of confession which he will press up against but isn't yet brave enough to break through.

Afterwards, I go downstairs to begin dinner. Peter returns from the club, sweaty and light—whoever he's played, he's won. I send him upstairs to tell Wally to wash up. We take our seats at the table: by now, everything has become routine, though some nights, for a thrill, we sit in one another's places, just to see what it feels like. We begin eating—pesto, cold chicken breast, salad. Peter gets up and slides open the living room's glass door, to get a breeze. Walter has a second helping of chicken. There comes a sweet moment, after eating, the three of us sitting there, before any of us begin wondering what we are going to do for the rest of the night.

The phone rings. We all start around like frightened deer. This is such a rare sound, none of us quite remembers what to do. Finally, Walter—through television, the most clued in—gets up, but I beat him to the phone.

It's Sidney. "Joan? We've just finished up dinner over here, and we wanted to know if you and the boys wanted to come with us to Snowflake later on." Snowflake is the town soft ice cream place.

"How soon?"

Sidney says, "An hour?"

"I'll ask the boys." Covering the mouthpiece, I look into the dining room. Peter and Walter are both staring at me, fascinated. Wide-eyed. "Fellas? Do you want to go to Snowflake with the Coltons?" Sartre says we know the answer to every question we ask.

We pull into the neon-lighted lot of the ice cream place seventy minutes later. They've brought the dog along, and we have to leave all the windows partially open, to allow him air. Sidney, as we are walking away from the car, explains, "We had to bring him with us: he can't bear being alone." I've always thought you can tell a lot about people's neuroses from the neuroses of their pets. Samantha, Sidney's eleven-year-old daughter, is also along. She looks and acts like a female version of Sidney, walking with that same little confident bustle.

All ice cream places are the same: the flies hovering around overfull trash cans (people can never manage to get their dishes actually in the garbage), the flickering fluorescent tubes, the teenagers (the same ones who later will leave tire tracks on the beach) languishing on car tops, laughing. Sidney has made it clear he's paying—a relief—so I find us a table, and he goes to the counter with the children. They return bearing napkined cones of cherry, chocolate dip, and vanilla. Even Sidney has gotten something, an ascending twirl of vanilla with a light coating of nuts like a swipe of eraser dust; an architect's spare, clean cone. I watch as they suck and slurp. Peter looks at Walter's ice cream with the suspicion that his younger brother might somehow have gotten something better than he did. Sidney, Peter, and Alex start talking about sports. Walter doesn't care much about sports, but—since he knows the most up-to-date box scores—he joins right in. Samantha, my companion adrift in this sea of maleness, looks at me with (already) a woman's look of frank amusement. Her mother's influence, surfacing through the Colton bravado. What strikes me is how Sidney, who after all has a stable relationship with his children, is able to calmly ignore one of them—without her even minding—whereas I have to always attend to my children, stickily mediating between them, an ideally anxious hostess with just two guests.

They've finished eating, so we all get up, successfully throw away napkins and half-cones, and walk back to the car. The same teenagers stare at us, with their little edge of menace—they're the real East Hampton people, and they regard us with the hostility of the citizens of a subjugated nation-state. The car, in our absence, has developed that sweaty, overheated smell of dog, and when I slip my shoes off, the rubber mat feels sandy under my feet. This is what vacations are about—changes in texture and smell, noticeable textures and smells. In New York, you never notice anything; everything feels and smells the same.

Sidney drives us back to our house, a white wood-and-glass concoction sitting on a patch of bare earth that has never been landscaped. The couple who built it divorced before its completion. From the clothesline in back, our bathing suits hang like the colors of a new nation. I look around and think that this is what my father's death has bought: a house the real estate lady described as "sparsely furnished" (I didn't mind, it was the only one in her listings I could afford), a station wagon, our tans. The dog comes inside with us and starts sniffing around at everything, this being to him a whole new planet. In the hallway light Walter, who hasn't been outdoors in a week, looks cruelly pale. "You guys want to come up and watch TV?" he asks the other kids.

Samantha turns to her father. "Can we, Dad?"

"If it's okay with Joan," Sidney says.

I say, "Fine by me." Everyone goes running upstairs, even the dog, his claws making tick-tack sounds against the steps. I wonder if Sidney has planned this out before: is he going to come in, or go home and pick up his kids later?

"Mind if I come in?" he asks, from the doorway.

"Please do."

The living room is also sparsely furnished. We sit down on the couch, Sidney reclining in a big-bodied way, spreading his legs and resting a forearm on each thigh. He smells of salt, there's still some sand in his hair. He hasn't washed since the beach, calculatedly sexy. My tension is back: We have to think of more things to say. It's Kadima for adults, keeping the ball in play. Sidney leads off with, "Been painting much?"

"No. Since the boys moved to Hartford, I wanted to spend as much time as possible with them now."

Sidney looks around. "Would there be room to paint in here even if you wanted to?"

This insult sort of endears Sidney to me—it shows, perhaps, that he's not so accomplished at this after all. "Probably not," I say. The subject makes me nervous—it seems cheap to use my profession as small talk, a betrayal, somehow. "I thought the porch for a while, but now I see it wouldn't have worked. What's funny is that I haven't missed painting at all. Structured time, yes. But not the actual painting."

Sidney absorbs this confession with a nod. He looks at me: his eyes are not totally blue, but like scallop shells are mottled with tiny, mixed-in lines of white and gray. "It's not so strange," he says. "It's like not missing a person you're supposed to be in love with. What do you think of that?"

I shrug. Sidney crosses his legs and leans back—he's made his shot. "You know," he says, clearing his throat, "I used to paint."

"Really?"

"Don't laugh," he says. "I even had a loft, where I used to go late at night to do my evil work. My wife thought I was using it as an excuse for seeing other women. In the end, I did end up bringing Cynthia over, which made the whole thing into a cover, but for a while I was honestly debating between painting and architecture."

"What were your paintings like?"

He looks around for paper. "I could show you," he says. I get up, bring paper and pencil from my bedroom. Then I clear the shells and beach detritus the boys and I have collected from the coffee table to give Sidney a clear space. This is more like it. I feel comfortable, back in my parental role, supervising projects. When Sidney begins to draw, I have the urge to praise him, as if he were one of my sons. "They were more or less like this." He draws thin lines, crosshatching the back. It looks like early Diebenkorn, very sixties.

"They're nice," I say.

"Thanks," he nods. "After the divorce, I gave up the loft. I should have held on to it, it would have been a sound investment." He laughs. He starts a fresh page. He draws lines and more lines. I watch, my head by his shoulder. In the center is an empty, boxy space. "Cynthia never liked my work either. *She* saw it as a dodge, too." Now he draws a little man-shaped figure in the center, draws lines in front of it. The lines suddenly take on the exact look of prison bars. Sidney draws a word balloon coming out of the man's mouth, saying, "Please help me." He looks up at me, with a frightened look of triumph, laughing, daring me to decode this.

Bleary-eyed, his children emerge from Walter's bedroom upstairs, as if from an opium den. Walter and Peter trail behind them. Only the dog seems unaffected by this blitz-krieg of television. He scrabbles downstairs. Samantha comes into the living room, touches Sidney's arm. "We're ready, Dad."

We get up. "What'd you see, Sam?" he asks.

"*Eight Is Enough*. Dad, why can't we have a television?"

He drops a hand onto her shoulder. "You watch enough in the city."

We all amble back towards the area in front of the door. Poor Walter looks frustrated: it must have been quite an effort for him, watching with the other kids, not being able to nose around between stations. *Eight Is Enough*, like *The Brady Bunch* and *The Partridge Family*, is a show about a large, happy family. All the children I've met are susceptible to these sorts of shows, though families are exactly the things everyone in my generation wanted to slip away from and avoid. Alex asks, "Can we come back later, Dad? Peter says there's going to be a Mets game."

"Some other time, Al," his father says. "Now we'd better go. We're keeping the Freelys up."

Sidney opens the door, and his children file out under the bridge of his arm, Alex steering the dog with a single finger under its collar. "I'll be out in a minute," he calls to them.

Peter and Walter say good night and go up to their rooms. Sidney looks at me frankly, the Jewish pirate up close. He might be proposing a raid. "What are you doing later?" he asks.

"I thought I might read. Why?"

"Well," he says, "if you feel like it, why don't you come over to my house? You know which one it is, don't you?"

"I've seen it from the road."

"We could have some wine, talk. Very relaxed. You don't have to call either way. Okay?"

Not knowing what to say, I smile and nod back. Sidney touches my cheek with the side of a little half-fisted hand and walks out. This is what we have in common—a vocabulary of gestures from forties movies. I hear him walking across the driveway, opening and closing his door, and then I hear his car starting and driving out onto the street. I wash the dishes from dinner, which up to now have been soaking in sudsy water. I sponge the dining room table clean of crumbs. All the while, I'm thinking over Sidney's offer: should I go to sleep, or should I go sleep with Sidney? I want to wake Peter and Walter for a family discussion. I try to think of who I could call in New York. My mother, I know, would advise me never to go out walking at night, no matter what the circumstances. What if the kids wake up and wonder where I am?

Peter, sleeping, looks curiously defenseless without his glasses. His eyelids are squinched up, as if he is playing some difficult sport even in his sleep, and his breath is heavy. I close his door. Walter sometimes stays up to forbidden hours, so as to give us the latest weather report first thing in the morning; I half expect to see a bar of light under his door now, but there's nothing. I open it, and he's asleep, deep in the shadows of his room. I move to close the door. "Mom?" he calls, his voice dry. I go back into his room and sit on his bed. He makes a space for me by moving his legs to one side.

I put my hand on his forehead. You forget how warm boys' skin gets when they are asleep.

"What's up, sweet?" I ask.

"I was sleeping," he says, with Cronkite solemnity. "I had fun tonight," he says. He opens his eyes, and this adds a new color to both sides of his face, small ovals of white. "I read Dad's postcards," he says, looking at me.

I keep my hand on his forehead. "How was the writing?" I ask.

He laughs. "I don't miss him at all," he says. And, in the dark room, I feel both of us sliding up against that barrier once again, so that it's only the darkness between us, a little translucent shield through which we can see each other's gray skin. "I wish he'd stay in Europe. I don't want to leave Springs."

I kiss him on the forehead. Talking to Sidney has made me forget, almost, this form of speech, parent-to-child. Walter, following mental tracks of his own, asks, "Why haven't you opened your bank statements?"

"They just came today," I say. In the darkness, I feel him responding to this lie. "Did you open them?" I ask.

"Well, they'd been there so long."

"Don't tell me what they said." He nods, under my hand, and, with my example of cowardice, we both seem to have stepped back away from the division. I pat his forehead. "I was thinking of going for a walk, and I didn't want you or your brother to worry. I'm glad you're awake."

Walter looks at me with perfect clarity. "Will you be back by morning?"

I laugh. "Of course. What do you think? Don't worry." I kiss him on the cheek. At the door, he calls, "Mom?" again.

"What, sweetheart?"

He takes a breath. "It's going to be seventy-seven degrees

217

tomorrow, with a chance of showers in the late afternoon.''

I close the door and go downstairs, outside. It's still warm out. The crickets are making their nighttime racket, and the road looks slick and black. There's that wonderful humid, vaguely mildewy smell the nights here get. In the other houses, figures sit flickeringly illuminated by bursts of television. I'm the only person out. On Accabonic I turn left. It's a ten-minute walk to Sidney's, and I can clearly picture his house: the bare wood walls, the deck, his Volvo outside, the orange light in the living room window framing his mustached reading head. A few insects, out for the evening also, hover around me. I'm thinking about Sidney: If I go, we'll cheat on his girlfriend. She'll come out on weekends, and I'll make myself scarce, and then on weekdays he'll see me. This is how my generation is—slipping away from any semblance of family, farther and farther until finally we're alone. Plus, how will Peter and Walter react, Sidney always coming over? I'm not worried, but it will have an impact.

By the old graveyard, roughly the halfway point between the two houses, I've realized I don't want to go. I want to talk to Walter about his father's postcards, about his father. I pause for a second. This is the graveyard where Jackson Pollock is buried; all summer, I haven't been out to visit it. In the night, the tombstones are as white as Walter's eyes in his room. The walk home is quicker. It seems like I'm back on my street, up on my unlandscaped lawn, opening my door, in less than a minute. Inside, I think I see a figure— Walter, I hope, congratulating me on having done the right thing, come to talk about his problems in Hartford, to tell me he's coming back to New York—and I hear a noise, but it's only Sidney's drawings, rustling in the sudden breeze between the patio and the open front door.

ABOUT THE AUTHOR

David Lipsky was born in New York City. He graduated from Brown University in 1987, and received his M.A. from Johns Hopkins. His stories have appeared in *The New Yorker*, *Mississippi Review*, *The Boston Globe Magazine*, and other magazines, and have been anthologized in *Best American Short Stories 1986*. He has received numerous awards for his writing, including a MacDowell Fellowship, a Henry Hoyns Fellowship, and the Henfield/*Transatlantic Review* Award. Mr. Lipsky lives in New York City. This is his first book.